The
FALL *of* DREAMS

RYAN LASALLE

Printed in the USA

Copyright © 2018 Ryan LaSalle

Winterset Books 2018

wintersetbooks.com

ISBN-13: 978-0-692-04007-2

For my children

CONTENTS

ACKNOWLEDGMENTS

My mother, who showed me the power of imagination
My wife, who inspired me to finish what I started
My sister, who was my sounding board from the beginning
My sister, who encouraged me with her music
My father, who gave me my love of books

The FALL of DREAMS

CHAPTER ONE

PETER, ALONE

The school day was down to the last half hour but even thirty minutes was all too much for Peter Engel. While the other students diligently worked on their math tests, Peter was hanging on by a thread. His slight physical appearance was no more unique than his brown hair that was grown to the length of the season, and his sweater was nearly the same brown color, although it was a little long in the sleeves so that most of the time, just his fingers showed. It was late October, but the weather hadn't even started to ponder the thought of winter. However, change was coming. The hints could be felt in the mornings where the crisp air fingered its way over the landscape and didn't let go until midday, and there were more clues in the afternoon when the sunlight looked pale as its travelling arc was falling on the horizon more and more with each passing day.

Ms. Fetterly, a stout woman of fifty, watched over her fifth-grade class to make sure everyone was doing their own work. She paced from one side of the class to the other, scanning the rows. All of her students were making progress on their math test, except one. At the back of the class, Peter was hunched over his desk like a lifeless puppet. He hadn't slept in days and the lack of rest went well beyond looking a little tired. He was so exhausted that he teetered on the verge of collapse. He was fighting the drowsiness with every determined thought—trying to concentrate on the numbers in front of him, but it was little use. He studied and knew the material, but his knowledge wasn't enough. All of his senses were slipping under. His pencil hung loose in his grip as he rubbed his eyes and though he tried to concentrate on the next question, his vision was starting to dim. The four became a nine which blurred next to the eight and soon all the lines seemed to blend together.

Peter pulled back, thinking the movement would keep him awake, but as soon as he saw the twitching of other students scribbling calculations, he slumped back to his original position. The furious scratching of pencils next to him formed a lulling sound that beckoned him to sleep. He heard the clock strike down another minute and everything in the room became an incomprehensible canvas of shapes.

The shapes gave way to darkness and the darkness parted like curtains across a stage. The classroom was gone and a sharp band of light hit his eyes from above. He was no longer in his classroom. Instead, he found himself in a small room made of tightly woven branches where traces of dust swirled, illuminated by the shafts of light cutting through the openings. He tried to pull himself up but couldn't move; he was on a wood table with his hands pulled over his head, bound by crude rope that was fastened to the sides. Outside, there was a faint voice just beyond the doorway.

"No, he'll come to, but we mustn't frighten him. He's not like the others. His thoughts are very alive here. He could help. But how? She is very hungry."

Peter's eyes grew wide at hearing the word hungry. He pulled again on the rope and his right hand gave way, retreating through the knot a little more. Whoever was speaking, they were now nearing the doorway. Peter pulled again, straining hard against the knot until his hand slipped through. He then used his free hand to loosen the other knot and he rolled off the table and crawled through a window at the back of the hut.

The light outside was blinding, a golden hue that

made him immediately shut his eyes. He opened them slowly letting his vision adjust and a new world came into focus. A world where bright orange pumpkins of all sizes sat in their nurseries laced in wilting vines. The ground was dry and lumpy and it carried with it the spiced dusty smell of fall. Beyond the pumpkin patch, rows of skeleton trees with their bare fingered branches watched over the squash and beyond that more trees, packed so tightly, that they formed a textured gray where tree could not fathom tree. Peter looked up. A painted sky hovered over the forest in a mix of yellow, orange, and red.

Then he heard her voice again. "No. No! Where is he?" Peter dashed over the dusty path into the trees. He slipped behind a wide trunk then slowly craned his head around it, peering back. There, a long spindly figure searched near the hut. She was draped in a long glossy garment of the darkest blue and her arms dangled at her sides like broken branches. Peter held his breath, watching her tread weightlessly along the path as her skeletal frame undulated beneath the wide blue brim of her hat. Her head swayed side to side, dipping occasionally to peer in between the trees. She was a frightening figure…and yet her movements were strangely graceful. As if sensing Peter's gaze, she stopped to listen, and then slowly turned, about to reveal her face…

Peter's pencil shook intensely at the end of his

fingers until it broke free and fell. It made a quick *crack* as it kicked off the floor. At the sound, he was jolted awake. He felt disoriented and afraid. Afraid to discover where he was. The sound of pencils scratching reminded him. The math test. Slowly, he raised his head to find Ms. Fetterly staring directly at him with an expression that betrayed her concern.

* * *

Dr. Avery's office was a supply room until two years ago when the school decided to give the district's psychologist a permanent place of his own. The room seemed smaller than it was due to the fact there were no windows and the furniture was too large for the space. The heavy oak desk with plate glass over the top was impossibly clean without even a trace of dust daring to rest on its surface, and the two towering file cabinets on each side looked like sentries awaiting orders. On the side wall, there was only one thing that seemed out of place and that was a large square electrical panel that made a low but constant *buzzing* and the shelves that once carried industrial cleaning supplies were now used for Dr. Avery's books. However, the real focal point of the office was Dr. Avery's formidable framed diploma that loomed behind him like a work of art in a museum.

The psychologist was not particularly old, forty-three to be exact, but many thought he was nearing retirement. This might have had something to do with the full beard he wore or the painful sighs he made every time he rose out of his chair. It was as though the tightness of the room or perhaps the *buzzing* of the electrical panel was making the doctor increasingly irritable.

Peter sat quietly in the chair watching Dr. Avery make notes. It wasn't the first entry in the boy's file, but it was very similar to the last. The scratching of Dr. Avery's pen and the noise of the electrical panel were the only sounds. As the seconds turned to minutes, Peter started to feel tired again. He blinked his eyes a few times and rubbed his forehead.

Abruptly, Dr. Avery dropped his pen and settled back in his chair. He didn't look so much concerned about Peter's condition as much as he seemed weary of the routine altogether.

"Ms. Fetterly says your grades are dropping. You haven't done very well on your tests or quizzes. You fell asleep in the cafeteria last week and today during a math test," he said. "I called your mother and she's very concerned. She told me that you haven't slept at night for several days and she thinks you're still afraid."

Dr. Avery waited a few moments to see if Peter would offer anything, but he didn't. Instead, Peter sat so quietly that Dr. Avery was starting to feel like he was talking to himself.

"Fears are a part of growing up, but we can't let them control us. Especially, if the fears are of things imagined, not real. Do you want to tell me what's going on?" Dr. Avery paused. "Peter?"

Letting his glance dip, Peter found himself staring blankly at his own file. Dr. Avery wrote like an architect so that each letter was clearly drawn and it was fairly easy to make out some of the words upside down. Peter could see the dates written along the margin—other times when he was sent to the psychologist to talk about why he was falling asleep in class. He focused on the first entry and remembered the first time he met with Dr. Avery which was the last time he had talked about his troubles to anyone.

Dr. Avery remained in the back of his chair and wasn't nearly as persistent in his questions as he had been during previous meetings. He was starting to think that Peter was playing games with him and he wasn't amused. Rather than try harder, he simply put a scaling finger to his cheek and said, "You're ten years old Peter. Ten."

Peter gave no indication of the shame he felt or his growing anger over the last comment but instead let his mind wander off, away from tightness of the room.

* * *

Susan, his mother, arrived shortly after and talked with the Dr. Avery inside his office. Peter sat in the waiting room just outside staring at an art project of not-so-carefully traced paper hands made by Ms. Kilwinger's first grade class. He let his glance drift over to someone else in the room. A girl, who was a little older, looking anxious…sitting on her hands, pulling them back up, rubbing her palms, then sitting on them again. Peter didn't know her name but remembered seeing her in line with the sixth graders, next to his class when they would assemble for activities. She caught his glance and held it for a moment. She was lanky, with refined features, straight brown hair, and crystalline eyes. For a moment, Peter couldn't break the glance because he was lost in the strange color of her eyes. When he finally realized he was staring, he looked down for a moment and then back up. She was looking away then she looked back at him again.

At first, Peter could only hear a few sporadic words, but then somehow, he focused and could hear Dr. Avery pretty clearly.

"Didn't say anything—"

"—like he's ashamed," his mother finished.

"Maybe. Unfortunately, there's little I can do if he's unwilling to talk about it. I've really tried."

Peter caught himself shaking his head a little at the last remark. Dr. Avery didn't care as much as he liked to let people think.

"We just don't know what to do anymore."

There was a pause. His mother was standing next to the door, up against the frosted glass window. She looked tired herself. Peter thought about how he was to blame for all of this. Why couldn't things be like they used to be? Why couldn't he be like all the other kids?

"Here. It's an option." Dr. Avery handed his mother a piece of paper. Peter knew what it was.

"I'm sorry, no."

"It's not habit forming. He needs help."

"He does, but no thank you."

"Well, there are other options. Special programs that he might benefit—"

"—You mean a different school?"

"We have to consider other ways to help him. Other ways to reach him."

"No, he likes it here. At least, he did, before all this started," his mother said.

Peter listened intently. Another school? Dr. Avery didn't want to help; he just saw Peter as a problem and wanted to pass him off to someone else. Peter sank lower as he thought about trying to start over. A few kids in his class teased him about falling asleep but most left him alone. He didn't have many friends, but he had met a few new people. It was a start. He closed his eyes, imagining what would happen, but then a noise caught his attention and he looked up to find that the girl had unlatched the window in the waiting room. She pushed it up, stepped onto the seat of the chair, and climbed out. Sitting on the window sill, she looked back at Peter and offered him a hand.

"Ready?" she asked.

Peter pointed to himself, still unsure that she meant him. Peter glanced around as though he needed to be reminded that they were the only ones in the room.

"Let's go," she whispered.

In seconds, they were outside and across the schoolyard.

CHAPTER TWO

THE "NATURE" OF FEAR

Sarah ran along a narrow path with Peter stumbling a few yards behind, struggling to catch up. The decision to leave was so quick and impulsive, that by the time Peter was outside, he almost didn't realize he actually did it. He had left the school and run away with a girl he didn't even know. Both were a first. Wait, what am I doing? he thought, finally coming to his senses, as though the last minute had been lived by someone else and not him. They went to the edge of the playing field, through the break in the fence at the wall of trees. They slipped into the woods along a well-worn path. Autumn color blurred past and soon they were out of sight of the school. The warmth of the hard shafts of light, and the touch of cool in the shadows created a contrast that could be felt. A sharp discernable dividing line between spaces. Peter slowed and started thinking about his mother entering the waiting room to find him gone.

"Wait. I should go back."

Sarah stopped. "Did you really want to stay there?" she asked.

Peter thought for a moment. Dr. Avery. The math test. A new school.

"No," he said flatly.

"Well, neither did I."

Sarah continued along the path. The ground sloped down a few feet and suddenly there was a heaviness in the air. Peter followed, thinking about what she said, and why she was waiting outside Dr. Avery's office.

"Why?" Peter asked.

Sarah stopped again almost grudgingly. "That was the point of leaving, so we wouldn't have to talk about it." She looked away, far off. "I'm tired of talking about it." She turned and started to climb up the side of a large gnarled tree. Sarah reached a fork in the trunk and crouched there with the ruins of an abandoned tree house looming above her.

A leaf filled breeze brushed her shoes and touched her hair and as soon as Peter saw it, he felt it too. There was a lasting gaze where no one knew what to do or say. Maybe an entire story passed between their glance and maybe nothing but puzzlement touched them both.

"I'm Sarah."

"Peter."

"You're in...fifth, right?" she asked.

Peter nodded. "I've seen you before. You're in art class after me."

"Mr. B's," she said.

Peter kicked the leaves in front of him not sure of what to say next. Sarah started to climb higher into the ruins of the treehouse.

"Where are you going?" Peter asked.

"Left something up here yesterday. At least I hope I did. Be right back."

Sarah disappeared behind an opening in the crooked tree house.

Peter lifted the collar of his sweater up around his chin as late afternoon descended on the forest. A few yards off, Peter heard a rustling among the leaves. He thought it must be a bird or cat, but he jumped back just the same. From behind a fallen limb, a big brown squirrel scurried onto an old jagged stump and pushed his nose up into the air. Peter smiled and fished in his pocket for a small piece of granola. He pulled it out of the wrapper and tossed it to the squirrel. The animal ran away, frightened, leaving the small bit of rolled oats and molasses to disappear into the leaves.

Peter watched the tops of the trees, their branches bending in the wind, then trying to regain their center. Behind a swirl of colored leaves, he spied a small stick caught between two branches. As the small whirlwind pushed back, the force dislodged the stick allowing it to drop to the ground.

Peter took no more than a few seconds to see what it might really be. Not a stick but something else. On bended knee, he reached for the thin object, switching it so that the slender pointed end was at the top. Then, like a minstrel of imagination, he waved it about slaying every troll and witch that dared come near. They, of course, did not exist, but watching his thrusts, dives, and ducks, one might think he was truly responding to something he could see.

Peter's mind was a wild and willing engine given free rein to create whatever it desired or dared; a device that too often had threatened to play tricks on its possessor. He was the creator, but with every gesture, he became a reactor to that self-discovered world. It was pure adventure even if sometimes his imagination mimicked the wind and ran away with him.

Peter shook his head and continued through the trees waving the stick in front of him. His shoes crushed the soft leaves with little sound until he stepped on a small dry twig buried underneath and there was a *snap*. He spun around and thrust the stick backward.

"Nice moves."

Startled and embarrassed, Peter dropped the stick as he discovered that Sarah was behind him. Out in the open, without a good excuse, he looked vulnerable.

"Just a walking stick," he mustered unconvincingly. "What were you looking for anyway?"

"Just this." Sarah revealed a raggedy hooded sweatshirt dusted with leaves. "I spend a lot of time out here. It's a good place to think."

Peter looked around again. They were surrounded by long shadows from the late afternoon sun. "Really, I should get back. They'll be worried," he said.

Sarah examined him closely for the first time and could see the effects of insomnia—his dark ringed eyes, and his pale drawn face.

"Jeez. What happened to you?"

"I don't sleep," Peter said looking away.

"Yeah, I heard them talking. Not at all?"

"Not much."

"Why?"

"I thought we weren't going to talk about it."

"You started it."

"It's not safe."

"Sleep isn't safe?" she asked.

"No. My dreams are very real."

"You mean vivid?"

"No, I mean real, so I try to stay awake. It's hard to explain."

Peter stepped away, ashamed. There was an awkward silence. Sarah wasn't sure if she wanted to ask any more questions from someone she really didn't know. However, she had never met someone who didn't sleep and she found herself a little curious about this.

"Well, I have a meeting every week," she said uncomfortably. "They pretend to understand, but they don't. They want to talk about it, but I don't. They're paid to listen, but they don't care." Sarah shrugged. "Why? It won't bring him back."

"Your brother…?" Peter asked.

Sarah nodded solemnly.

"I heard. I'm sorry."

"To be honest, I don't like my dreams either. No place is safe," she said. Sarah trudged on, navigating the path, with Peter trailing.

"I really should get back home," he protested.

"I know."

"You don't have to show me the way."

"Well, I got you into this. I feel like I should help get you out. Back to the main road?"

Peter nodded.

"It's this way," she said.

Sarah watched her footing on the uneven ground then pulled her attention back to the stretch of forest in front of her. She plodded on not looking back. Light was fading fast. Peter stood alone watching Sarah walk deeper into the woods—her thin frame navigating the protruding branches.

"Wait up," he said.

Peter caught up to her and walked alongside, sometimes a few yards ahead just to prove that he also knew the way. The sun was down and darkness was upon them. They moved in and around large twisted trees with towering dark branches. The leaf dusted floor was getting blacker.

"At least it's Friday. Almost Halloween. All kinds of strange things out tonight. I'm sure of it," Sarah said glancing up at the canopy.

"Just as scary as any other night," Peter countered.

Sarah stopped suddenly. "What was that?" she said with wild eye bewilderment. Peter froze. He scanned the woods. Sarah watched him intently. She made a mischievous grin right before she reached over the top of his shoulder with her index finger and tapped him. He jumped.

"You are scared of the dark." Sarah smirked a little but didn't laugh. Peter was embarrassed but his silence revealed that it was true. He was scared. He played in the woods all the time but never this late.

"So what scares you?"

"Imagination."

"I don't get it."

"Witches. Monsters. The usual."

"Then don't believe in them."

"I don't, or I didn't. It's just that, when I close my eyes, or even when I'm asleep, I can see them very clearly."

"So your imagination is too good?" she asked. Peter shook his head, maybe didn't feel quite so alone.

"I'm scared of the same things. The dark," Sarah said.

"It's stupid." Peter jumped off the stump and pushed on.

"No, it's not," she returned. "I'm scared of the same things. It's just that we can't see in the dark. Our minds create things that aren't really there." Sarah passed Peter on the path and stopped at the edge of the road. A car passed. Headlights struck the two traveler's eyes. The last flicker of light was almost gone.

"Gives me chills just thinking about it but goosebumps aren't good for you." She wrapped her arms around herself and pulled tight. "You can't stay awake forever. At some point, you'll have to sleep and confront your dreams, your nightmares. Here, I remember a trick my mother told me. She said, if you do find yourself in a bad dream, just remember that you'll always wake up when you fall and hit the ground. At least I do." Sarah smiled.

"Thanks," Peter said.

Sarah kissed him gently on the cheek. "For luck" she said, then she scampered over the road into another stretch of trees. Peter seemed stunned by her touch for a moment. He watched her vanish from view and then looked to both sides, realizing he was alone in the advancing darkness.

The sun had just gone down and the road was quiet in the half light of dusk. Leaves danced across the pavement, chasing one another in curled lines, settling into piles for a brief repose only to have the wind send them into another flight of confusion.

Strange shadows surrounded him as he maneuvered through the trees. He heard noises, sticks *cracking*, the *caw caw* of a crow from above. The sounds became distorted. They sounded sinister, horrific, and chilling. Peter ran faster.

CHAPTER THREE

THE UNINVITED GUESTS

Beyond the path of leaves, the Engel home, sat just behind the first row of trees off the main road. It was old. Weathered shingles draped over the sides and the window frames lost a little more color every season, paint chip by paint chip.

Peter ran out of the woods, passing the woodpile and the small shed at a brisk pace. Golden grasses dotted the tattered fence line dividing the forest from the family's loosely drawn backyard. Along the sidewall of the shed, were two rusty bikes, an old plastic bat, and a dingy red ball that looked as though it had seen too many days outdoors. As he approached the house, he saw a police car in the driveway, and knew he was in trouble.

* * *

Peter sat at the kitchen table, his arms pulled close, and his hands in his lap. The police officer had left. Peter's father, Tom, stood near the sink with his arms folded, looking down at the floor. Susan sat next to Peter at the kitchen table. No one looked pleased.

"I'm glad you're alright, but that was very dangerous. We didn't know where you were, or what had happened," Susan said.

"I'm sorry," Peter said, not making eye contact.

"Then why did you do it?" Susan asked.

"I don't know."

The feeling Peter had when he was in Dr. Avery's office came over him again. The feeling that he needed to lock everything up. He didn't want to talk about it. He just wanted to be left alone.

"What do you mean, you don't know?" she persisted.

Peter didn't respond.

"Answer your mother," Tom said. But still nothing from Peter.

"The no talking treatment again?" Tom looked to Susan. "I can't do this. He just tunes us out. How are we supposed to help when he won't say anything?"

Tom walked out of the room visibly frustrated. Susan looked over at Peter and placed her hand on his.

"Why won't you talk to us Peter? I can't see you like this. Help me understand what's wrong," she said with a tear in her eye. Peter sank lower. He didn't want to worry his parents. He didn't want to cause his mother to cry, but he didn't know where to start or how to explain what had happened.

* * *

Night settled in. Tom and Susan talked quietly in the kitchen after dinner. Light from the television flickered on the walls of the living room. Peter glanced away from the screen and stared up at the window just long enough to see a few stray leaves swirling against the house. *The Wizard of Oz* came back from commercial and Lisa, his sister, who was six, and still pudgy, rolled over like a fuzzy caterpillar, crowding her brother. Annoyed, he yanked her blanket off and pushed back.

"Mom!" Lisa yelled.

"Peter," Susan warned standing in the doorway into the kitchen, "don't bother your sister." Lisa poked her head over the top of the couch to see. "He took my blanket and he's being mean."

"Give it back to her."

Peter handed the blanket back grudgingly. Lisa

snatched it quickly and pulled it close before her brother decided to change his mind.

"Are you sure you want to watch this?" Susan asked. Lisa glared at her brother and taunted, "Yeah, flying monkeys! Aren't you scared?" Peter gave Lisa another push, but she held her ground. "Mom!" Lisa yelled again.

For the most part, Peter and Lisa got along, until one of them was cranky or bored. Usually the latter was the start of many fights over nothing and while entertainment was the primary goal, it usually ended in someone getting their feelings hurt. Most of the time Peter was the one to stir up trouble, but his sister had learned a few tricks of her own.

Tom entered from the hallway after hearing the commotion and gave them both a stern look. "Alright, I'm breaking this up." He sat down between them in their makeshift nest. The siblings exchanged glances of blame then slowly turned their attention back to the movie. Their father was always the last straw. He worked long hours as an accountant, more so in the spring, and was usually too tired to do much of anything. This wasn't to say that he wasn't a good father but whatever he had to offer always came late. He was never much for playing with his kids, but he liked to watch television and thought it counted if he watched whatever they were watching.

Tom picked up the remote and turned to Peter.

"We're carving pumpkins tomorrow. Are you going to join us?"

Peter shook his head "no."

"Well, we got one for you. If you don't use it, I guess we'll just have to give it to Lisa." Lisa sent a delightful smile toward her brother who couldn't resist changing his answer. "I don't know. Maybe," Peter said.

"Any flying monkeys yet?" Tom asked.

"They're coming up," Peter answered.

Lisa curled up closer to her father. She knew when to get a jab in and she was feeling mischievous and bold. "I saw two outside tonight. They flew off with your pumpkin," she said to Peter with confidence.

Peter didn't take the bait. Seeing where this was going, their father decided to cut Lisa's plan short. "Everyone knows that flying monkeys don't like pumpkins."

"That's not in the movie," Peter said.

"What about witches?" Lisa asked.

"No, witches don't like them either," their father replied as though the whole topic of conversation was fact.

"Is that because it's a vegetable?" Lisa asked.

Susan, hearing the discussion, popped back into the living room and added, "Please, don't encourage them."

The movie ended. With Lisa asleep and Peter still

awake, Tom struggled to watch television. He closed his eyes every few seconds, taking deep breaths, as if to keep himself awake.

"Ready for bed?" Tom asked.

"Can't sleep." Peter's voice was just as awake as it was before.

"You can't nod off in math and not be tired now. It's been a few days." Tom said.

"I'm tired but..." Peter pointed to his head.

"Think only of sleep. Nothing else. It takes a little while, but it will work. If it doesn't, just count..." his father's voice dropped off.

"Count sheep? Won't work either," Peter said.

* * *

Tossing in bed, Peter tried to sleep but his mind was running. He imagined what the forest was like at night. Even if he did not believe in the creatures of fairy tales, his mind allowed his imagination to entertain them. He knew better, but the thought of a witch lurking outside in the yard still made him watch his window carefully. If he really didn't believe in any of these things, he wouldn't watch so closely. He wouldn't pull his feet up so tightly and he wouldn't lie so perfectly still. But he did all of this.

If he could just find sleep, he could escape these nightmares of the imagination, the daydreams of the night. Sleep would give him safety…unless it was one of *those* dreams. Like the one he had in school. Ones that weren't just like a vivid dream, but something more. Those were the ones that made him fearful of sleep. A night without dreams. That's what he really wished for. It would take the long hours of night and make them disappear and the next thing he would see is the light of morning telling him that all the darkness had passed. But the more he thought, the more awake he was.

As Peter's mind whirled, the sound of footsteps on the other side of his door grew closer. The door handle slowly turned and Peter's breathing increased. As the door pushed open, he pulled back to find his mother peering in. Looking tired herself, as though this was a nightly ritual, she sat at his bedside. When she saw that he was still awake and breathing heavily, she placed her hand on his forehead and sighed.

"Oh Peter, try to relax," she whispered.

"I'm trying," he answered in a weak voice, "I'm trying."

She soothed his arm until his breathing slowed and he was calm. The house creaked in the shadow laid hours like an old sailing ship restless in the harbor. They listened to the sounds and then his mother stepped lightly out of his room, closing the door behind her, wondering when her son would find rest.

Peter rolled over and tried to think of something

other than the forest. He counted to a hundred. He counted by tens and then fives. He counted by threes and sevens. After numbers, he named all the colors he could think of. First it was red, green, and blue but after a few minutes, it was cobalt, emerald green, cornflower, and aqua-marine.

The two dots on his clock continued to flash. He thought about Sarah and remembered their conversation. He stared at the clock again as the numbers began to blur. He whispered softly to himself, "I have to stay awake. I have to stay awake. I have to..."

He closed his eyes for a moment and started to see strange forms. He remembered the figure from his dream in class—the long figure walking along a dusty path. Who was she? Why was he captive? What was she talking about? The images slowly became clearer. Then, Peter heard a strange sound coming from the edge of his bed. He opened his eyes.

Slowly, he turned his head to feel a cold wind brushing across his cheek. His window was open...then the sound of chattering—something was in the room. The noises stopped for a moment then the quiet was broken by a monkey jumping onto the top of Peter's bed. Peter pulled back and hit his head on the wall.

The little creature stood about two feet high with wings that flapped intermittently. He jumped up and down angrily and chattered about something that Peter couldn't understand. More chattering was heard from under the bed and soon the rest of the group jumped up. Peter put his arms up defensively but the monkeys attacked in a frenzy of wing flapping. He found himself pinned down by strong little hands and one was pushing his face down into the mattress of the bed.

A large sack was produced and the monkeys forced him inside. They grabbed the corners and flapped their wings. Peter was flown out his window, across the yard, and over the trees. He noticed that there was a hole in the sack, a hole from which he could see glimpses of the forest below. Cold air whipped in through the opening making Peter squint his eyes. He pressed his fingers through the opening and noticed that the hole had become larger. Pretty soon he had two hands holding the tear, and like that, the tear grew, and suddenly, he dropped out of the bag, holding on by only a hand.

The monkeys were disoriented and some let go in all the commotion. The bag dropped down closer to the tops of the trees. More monkeys swooped in to grab onto Peter, but he let go and fell down through the branches. His stomach pressed upward and a falling sensation welled up in his throat. He hit the moist ground with a low muffled *thud*.

Peter opened his eyes to find the moon covered by

flashes of small moving bodies and flapping wings. The monkeys dropped under the canopy and split up to look for their missing prey. They batted through the branches and jumped from tree to tree investigating every shadow. One monkey landed on the ground and surveyed the forest floor. It ran along the leaves, kicking up a few here and there. The monkey then hopped onto a tree trunk, scampered along a main branch, and peered down from its perch.

The monkeys chirped angrily as they hunted, but after a few minutes, they moved to another stretch of woods. Soon the sounds of breaking branches and monkey cries faded and Peter lifted his head carefully over the big root to discover darkness and silence.

To his surprise, he was alive. His hands, arms, and legs seemed fine, and he didn't feel as though he was in any pain. In the stillness, he took his fingers and ran them across his cheek as though checking to see if he was real. He then touched the cold wet bark on an exposed root next to him. Nothing seemed real and yet everything was—his senses couldn't lie.

Peter pulled himself up and stood in a small clearing to discover an endless forest of trees half bare. A spattering of leaves moved like tiny specks of coal. Some still clung to the arms of the trees while others descended off the old timbers illuminated by blue light from above. The place seemed familiar to Peter, like the woods behind his house, but so far the inhabitants looked far from recognizable.

He stared up at the moon. There were a few streaked clouds to both sides, but the circular glow was clearly visible. He did not want to look at the forest but instead wanted to stare at the moon thinking its light was a beacon of safety. That if he looked at it long enough, all of this would end, but as soon as his mind began to draw the image of his home, his room, his bed, he saw something moving against the image of the moon. The monkeys were flying high above the forest—all of them, cutting across the bright sphere. Peter decided that if the monkeys were flying one way, he must go the other way.

It was difficult for Peter to tell exactly how long he had walked, but it felt like hours. He passed tree after tree over a musty forest floor covered with wet leaves that crushed softly under his feet. He was cold, from top to bottom, but he continued to walk in the direction of home, or what he thought was the direction of home.

After passing through a small patch of fog, Peter stopped and wrapped his arms across his chest grabbing his shoulders. He did not want to continue. He was exhausted, so he decided to sit on an eroded log and close his eyes. He wanted to go home, but now he found himself unable to clearly picture his house. The memory was fading and the harder he focused on it, the faster it disappeared.

Despair swept into his heart like the chilled wind that was starting to pick up in the forest. Leaves gathered up in the torrent and whipped by. The air was colder and Peter sensed something watching him. He turned and opened his eyes. Something was moving in the darkness. His eyes were accustomed to the shadow movement of the swaying tree branches but he knew this shape was different. The shadow was large. It was shortening, getting closer. His skin rippled. Without another thought, he ran. He ran fast, never looking back, never stopping.

CHAPTER FOUR

THORNE AND KEYS

Dawn's purple and orange light came with a light frost—a thin icy veil over the golden grasses and musty clumps of leaves. A new place awoke to the sound of fall. A new world of tangled forests and painted skies. A contained vision of limitless possibility.

Mr. Thorne's home was a towering tree house in the center of a five-acre clearing. It stood alone with its massive trunk expansive and pregnant with the first-floor rooms. From the fork at the top of the trunk, thick muscular branches stretched up and out, holding the upper floors, and in every remaining open space, there were little windows, awnings, and crooked chimneys. The tree house was encircled by an uneven picket fence that leaned forward in some sections and back in others. Its white paint was long since gone so that most of the pickets and rails matched the color of the dirt below. The yard was covered in sporadic piles of leaves that blended a warm palette of orange and red. Just inside the fence, were two small sheds each topped with a rusty red weather vane that turned stiffly under a constant wind. The entire plot was surrounded by a small wheat field, ready for harvest, and beyond that, the forest encroached with its gnarled bony trees.

Everything was quiet in the tree until Mr. Thorne was ready to work. He hunched under the doorway, stretched his arms, revealing that his gray frock coat was too small, then walked outside, heading straight for one of his little wooden sheds. He scratched his unruly hair and stared at the large black padlock hanging from the door of his tool shed.

Mr. Thorne put his hands on his hips and spun around. "Master Key," he yelled. Nothing happened. "Master Key!"

This time, Peter awoke, shook his head and blinked his eyes a few times. He was under a cloth tarp set over the wood pile at the edge of the yard. With some reservation, he lifted the tarp a little to view the scene. He could see Mr. Thorne pacing around and yelling "Master Key" in a fit of frustration.

Soon there was a new sound coming from another

shed that was shaped like a miniature house. Someone could be heard moving around inside. The sound changed and Peter could hear keys hitting one another. Mr. Thorne put his hands on his hips and stared impatiently at the small one room cottage next to the tree house. Abruptly, the door flew open and a tiny man, three feet tall, dressed in a colonial suit, complete with knee breeches and a dark tailcoat, jumped from the cottage and ran to the shed. Mr. Thorne gave a sharp look as Master Key hurried by. Peter noticed that the small man wore a pair of red earmuffs around his neck and he found this strange. Actually, he found the entire scene strange. He had explored many parts of the forest, but he had never seen anything like this.

"I need my saw," yelled Mr. Thorne.

"Yes Mr. Thorne. Right away Mr. Thorne." Master Key fidgeted through hundreds of keys hooked to his belt.

"Still waiting."

"Of course Mr. Thorne." The little man continued to look for the right key. His small pudgy fingers would insert an incorrect one then go quickly to the next.

"The right key."

"Right key coming right up Mr. Thorne."

Finally, after several tries, the lock opened and Master Key stepped aside. Mr. Thorne pushed the door inward and went inside. Peter could hear all sorts of *banging* from within. The clatter continued while the little man squinted and shuddered at every crash. Before long, all was quiet again. Mr. Thorne walked slowly out with nothing in hand.

"It's not there," he said mildly.

"Which saw? The big saw?" Master Key stretched his little arms out.

"No, that's the little saw." Mr. Thorne showed the same distance with his hands.

"The little saw?" Master Key brought his hands closer together.

"No, no, that's the tiny saw," Mr. Thorne said as he started to lose his composure once more.

"I can't make a big saw," said Master Key stretching his arms again in a futile attempt to show the length of the big saw. Mr. Thorne frowned, took a deep breath, then said slowly, "Well, where is the big saw?"

Master Key shrugged his shoulders. "I don't know Mr. Thorne."

Mr. Thorne erupted in anger. "Well go find it!" At the booming command, Master Key jumped into action and began scampering about the yard. He dodged left and zoomed right but still could not find the saw.

Peter glanced down and saw the tip of the saw in front of him. The other half was protruding out from under the tarp. He considered pulling it in or pushing it out but before he could act, he heard Master Key yell, "Here it is!"

Peter looked up to find the little man running right for the wood pile, directly toward him. Master Key pulled the tarp off and to his shock, found Peter huddled underneath.

With a loud scream, Master Key fell backward in alarm. Peter screamed too and tucked his head down between his knees.

"Ahhh, a witch! It's a witch!" yelled Master Key.

Mr. Thorne walked over to the woodpile calmly. "Hmm. A witch," he said. Peter slowly raised his head and took a peek at Mr. Thorne with one eye. Mr. Thorne stopped next to Master Key and studied the small huddled figure.

"Are you a witch?" Mr. Thorne asked.

Master Key got up and moved cautiously toward Peter. "Answer Mr. Thorne," he said while still keeping his distance.

"No," Peter said meekly.

"Is he oily?" asked Mr. Thorne. Master Key took a finger and cautiously poked Peter's right cheek. "Not greasy, but he's dressed funny."

Mr. Thorne walked to the side of the pile for a different view. "He's in pajamas," he observed.

"What are you doing in pajamas?" asked Master Key.

"He was sleeping in the woodpile," said Mr. Thorne. "How long have you been living in my woodpile?"

"Just last night sir. I'm lost." Peter said as he pulled himself up from his hiding place.

"You are not lost," Mr. Thorne countered.

"I am. I was in the forest. There something was chasing me last night." Peter gestured toward the trees. Master Key furrowed his brow and skewed his eyes, "A witch?"

"I don't know. I only saw a shadow," Peter said.

Mr. Thorne leaned closer. "Well, how did you get here?"

"I ran. I needed a place to hide and I found your tree house."

"Then you are not lost. You are at my tree house." Mr. Thorne opened his arms as if to indicate that the tree house was a grand place.

"Yes, but it's not my home."

"Well, where is your home?"

"That's just it. I don't know."

"Then, you are lost." Mr. Thorne said as he leaned back and grabbed onto the lapels of his coat.

"That's what I said," Peter answered sadly.

Mr. Thorne motioned to Master Key. "Interrogation."

Master Key turned to Peter. "All right, out of the woodpile. Move it." Peter stood up and steadied himself. At full height, he was a good foot and a half taller than Master Key. "I said, move it," said Master

Key as he pointed a large key at him in a threatening manner.

Peter was escorted inside the tree house. The first floor had a small kitchen and dining table next to the window but the rest of the room was fitted as a wood shop with many tools hanging on the walls. There were probably close to a hundred tools with each hung neatly in its own spot. There were mallets, hand saws, carving knives, chisels, and many different kinds of hand planes. Wood shavings covered the floor and Peter could see chairs, tables, cabinets, dollhouses, and wooden soldiers set neatly along the back wall. There were also many storage cabinets, complete with locks, set along the left wall.

Mr. Thorne sat Peter down in a chair in the center of the room and Master Key pulled his small chair from the dining table to be closer. Mr. Thorne shook his head at Master Key. "You can't sit now. We're just about to interrogate him."

"I wasn't going to sit. See?" Master Key stood on the seat of his chair to make himself taller. "Let the interrogation begin!" the little man yelled while pointing a finger at Peter. Mr. Thorne smoothed his mustache with his thumb and index finger mindfully then narrowed his eyes and pushed in close to the trespasser.

"Alright then. You are lost, but you are not a witch?"

"Yes," Peter said quickly.

"Are you a troll, bogey, or giant?" Mr. Thorne returned even faster.

"No, no, and no," Peter replied carefully as though giving thought to each one. Master Key nodded his head at the "giant" part and raised a level hand to indicate that Peter was significantly taller than he was.

"Then what are you?" Mr. Thorne opened his hand in front of Peter.

"I'm just a kid. A boy." Peter answered wondering if the obvious was the right choice.

"A boy," Mr. Thorne repeated, "and how old are you?"

"Ten."

Master Key excited with the questioning and eager to join in pointed his finger and exclaimed, "Ten what?"

"Ten years," replied Peter.

"Ten years!" exclaimed Master Key throwing his arms out as though he had uncovered important information. Mr. Thorne turned to his servant calmly, "Master Key..."

"Yes Mr. Thorne," he said, still excited.

"Quiet."

"Yes Mr. Thorne."

Mr. Thorne returned his questioning back to Peter. "So you are ten, what do you do?"

"What do you mean?" asked Peter.

"What is it that you do? Are you a farmer? A cobbler? A stable boy?"

"I go to school."

"You go to school?" replied Mr. Thorne in a condescending tone.

"Yes."

Mr. Thorne paused for dramatic effect then said slowly, "I am a carpenter and a craftsman. I have made everything that you see in this room. I have no use for students. I have no need for an apprentice. So you see, you cannot stay here, lost or not."

"But I don't want to stay here." Peter lowered his head and strengthened his voice as best he could.

"Well, you were here this morning."

"I just want to go home." Even without a clear image of what that word meant, he still knew he belonged home and this place was not it.

"But you do not know where that is." Mr. Thorne shook his head slightly.

"No. I thought I would ask you."

"How would I know where you live?" Mr. Thorne asked.

Everyone was quiet. Peter dropped his shoulders in a gesture of abandonment. Mr. Thorne stepped back. "The interrogation is over. You must go back to the forest."

For a brief moment, Peter felt a wave of sadness. Despair was taking over quickly, but he fought the impulse to show it. His eyes started to well up but instead of shedding a tear, he clenched his teeth. "I don't want to go back," he said.

Peter knew this with great certainty. So much had happened in the last few hours that "knowing" something was not certain, but he did not want to spend another night alone in the forest. He knew that more than anything.

"I'm sorry, but you can't stay here," Mr. Thorne said.

At the edge of the woods, Peter held an obligatory knapsack tied to a thin stick with Mr. Thorne waiting impatiently behind him. "Do you live this way or do you live that way?"

"He came from that way," said Master Key pointing toward the trees to his right.

"No, he came from this way," countered Mr. Thorne pointing in the other direction.

"Are you sure?" asked Master Key.

"I think it's that way," Peter replied.

"Right. That way," Master Key said.

Peter peered into the dark and threatening woods. They stood before him like an impervious wall. He could see just beyond the first row of trees then everything become a shade of gray. There was an eerie stillness and Peter again felt like something was watching him...waiting for him to venture deeper.

"So, that's it?" Peter asked.

"That's it. Goodbye," Mr. Thorne said.

Peter gave a fragile wave. Master Key waved back. Maybe this wasn't such a good idea, Peter thought. He crossed into the first row of trees. Large tangled limbs curved in every direction. Low fog drifted over the dank ground. Peter closed his eyes and took one step inward. He opened his eyes and the woods were still there. He stepped over the leaves and fallen twigs moving into the next row of trees. Soon the silence gave way to the voice of the woods. It was like a low threatening exhale. Cold and thick.

Peter kept watch out of the corner of his eye. He looked back. Nothing but trees. Soon, strange noises echoed in the woods. Again, he felt as though something was waiting out there. His mind was blank, his imagination a void, but a sinking feeling inside him continued to grow. He sensed there was something watching him.

* * *

Back in the kitchen of the tree house, Peter sat in a chair with Mr. Thorne looking down at him and Master Key looking up with long inquisitive stares.

"It might've been a witch. I don't know. I really didn't see it."

"Pitiful." Mr. Thorne circled Peter as he scratched his beard. "Trapped by your own fear. How can I make this clear? You can't stay here. So go."

Mr. Thorne pulled Peter out of the chair and nudged him toward the door impatiently.

"But I don't want to," Peter pleaded.

"Well, you can't stay here. You have no skill. You are of no use."

Another silence stopped the conversation, but Peter's mind was quick to acknowledge "skill."

"I can rake leaves."

"No use."

"I can cook meals."

"No use."

Peter looked around him at all the tools and items in the shop. Immediately, he had an idea.

"I can chop wood."

Mr. Thorne was about to answer when Master Key leaned over and whispered in his ear. After a short exchange, Mr. Thorne looked back at Peter and frowned a little.

"Hmm. All right. I will let you stay on the condition you chop wood out of the forest. Master Key is not terribly fast or good at the task, as he has pointed out."

"I don't care for it much," corrected Master Key.

"In the forest?"

"That's the offer."

"How far into the forest?" Peter asked nervously.

"Not far," Master Key answered.

"Only during the day. It is safe enough," said Mr.

Thorne.

"Will I have to sleep outside?"

Mr. Thorne shook his head and pointed to the ceiling. "No, there is an extra room. We will give you food and a place to sleep until you find or remember your way home. Are we agreed?" Mr. Thorne searched for a name.

"Peter...and yes, we're agreed," as he put out his hand.

An hour later, the task had already begun. Peter went to the edge of the wheat field pulling his cart with Master Key a few steps behind. At the spot of the first line of skeleton trees, Peter stopped and looked out across the small clearing. The sky was streaked in red and orange forming its own vibrant landscape above the horizon. He knew it didn't look real—it was like a thick saturated canvas placed back a few hundred yards.

No longer in pajamas, Peter wore a mix of Mr. Thorne's old clothes, which were too big, and Master Key's, which were too small. He squirmed in the new threads, trying to get comfortable, but it was little use.

"You're not stopping are you?" asked Master Key.

Peter looked back. "No. I'm going. Are you sure you wouldn't like to come?"

"No thank you. That's your job now."

"What's in the forest?" Peter inquired.

"Witches...all sorts of witches." Master Key made

lots of odd hand gestures.

"I heard that, but I don't believe in witches. The stuff of make believe." Peter leaned on the side of a tree trunk peering into the gray musty forest ahead of him.

"Peter, let me help you. If you find a cottage in the woods, stay away. If you see something you want, stay away."

"I said I don't believe in witches."

"That's ridiculous. Not believing in witches is like not believing in the tree you've put your hand on."

Peter stared at the bark his fingers were clutching. It felt real. For a brief second, his mind questioned his senses but the forest in front of him demanded consideration. He was about to enter into a dark web of trees where the only path seemed to disappear no more than a few yards inside. "For a little man, you sure try to make a big scare. Look, I said I don't believe in them, so stop trying to scare me."

Master Key looked up at Peter. "Scare you? I'm trying to save you. After all, if you don't come back, I'll have to get the wood and I don't care for it much."

Peter gripped the handles of the cart and pulled them up. "I have one more question. Why do you have earmuffs?"

"For sleep."

"To keep your ears warm?"

"No, not warm. Good luck Peter. Remember to

stay on the path. You'll see the stumps. Cut there and be careful."

"How far did you say it was?" Peter asked.

"I didn't say."

"Then could you say it now?"

"Not far."

Peter took a deep breath and took his first step. He again felt the shivers. Looking back, he could see Master Key and a glimpse of the horizon. The clouds moved in strange ways. He didn't know exactly what to make of Master Key's stories, but it bothered him. The reason he was here to begin with was at the clutching little hands and wings of monkeys that he never thought existed either.

The path winded into the woods and soon the sounds began to descend onto Peter. Sounds that leaves make as they strike one another. The sound of blackbirds slipping from tree to tree. He kept thinking that maybe he would emerge from the trees at any moment and find his home, but the forest never ended. The same gray bony trees obscured Peter's view in every direction. He tried to focus on the image of home and family, but it was gone. He knew only a vacant place in his mind where the memories were. It was feeling of loss, of knowing that something was missing, but not knowing exactly what.

After a few hours, the work was done. Peter had stacked logs on the back of the cart, each about six feet long. The clearing was like a dark room with trees to all sides that were so densely packed, they almost formed walls. He placed his hatchet at the front, and then tilted his ear toward a new sound coming from the other side of the cart.

"Nuts, I tell you."

"Who's there?" Peter asked.

"Who's that? Who asked that?"

Peter didn't see anyone. "I asked first. Show yourself," he said.

"Whoa, whoa, you expect me to go around?"

Peter realized that the voice was coming from the other side of the cart near the ground. He walked around to find a fat squirrel squatting on the pathway with a sack behind him.

"Move it!" the squirrel said.

Peter smiled and was not afraid at all. Rather, he was amused by the unusual character. "You're the fattest squirrel I've ever seen," he said.

"Yeah well, I gotta store nuts for the winter."

"Then what's in the sack?" Peter asked.

"Sack full of nuts, what'd you think it was?" quipped the squirrel.

"Maybe you should leave more in there."

"Hah. Hah. Look, I don't tell you how to hibernate. Are you going to move the cart?" the squirrel asked gruffly.

"I'll move the cart. Just calm down."

Peter wheeled the cart off the path so the squirrel could move by.

"Here." The squirrel threw Peter an acorn. "Crack it with your teeth," the squirrel said as he shuffled by, "Oh, that's it! Do you see it? I've found the one!"

Peter stepped back and turned, trying to figure out what the squirrel was excited about.

"Right there. That'll be perfect." The squirrel pointed to a hole in a tree about five yards away.

"What are you pointing to?" Peter was still confused by all of this.

"My new home," said the squirrel trying to move faster.

"That hole? Your new home?"

"I don't fit in my old one."

"Well, I hate to say it, but I don't think you're going to fit in that one either," Peter said.

"Yes I will. That's much bigger. Here, help me." The squirrel pointed to the heavy sack of food. Peter pitched in and helped pull. The squirrel slowly climbed up to the opening and started to push inward. He got about halfway when all forward progress came to a stop.

"Are you stuck?" Peter asked. A muffled voice came back, but Peter couldn't tell what the squirrel was saying. "I don't know what you said." Suddenly, the squirrel's tail went up and down steadily.

"Is that a yes?"

Peter decided that the signal was a "yes" and he pulled the large rodent back out.

Tired and short of breath, the squirrel mourned, "That's the third one today. The twelfth one this week." The squirrel lowered his head then reached into the sack for another acorn. "It's depressing. I'm never going to find a home and winter is almost here."

"Well, don't give up, but first, you need to give me...stop eating." Peter tried to pry the acorn from his hand. "Give it—"

The squirrel clutched his food tightly. "—Hey, it's all I have left."

Peter was getting mad. "Keep eating. Eat all of them. I don't care, but you'll never fit in there," he said pointing up to the hole. Peter went back to his cart and tried to dismiss the whole affair. He pulled the cart back onto the path and glanced down at his tools. Perhaps there was something he could do.

It only took a few swings of his hatchet to chip the sides of the opening of the hole to make it bigger. With a new step, the squirrel climbed in and Peter handed up the bag.

"Thank you, thank you, thank you. Here, have some more." The big rodent tossed more acorns at Peter, most of which fell to the ground.

"You're welcome, but stop, I don't want any more acorns."

"Well, what do you want? You helped me, maybe

I can help you," the squirrel said eagerly.

"Do you know how I can get home?" Peter asked.

The squirrel popped his head out of the hole. "That depends. Where do you live?"

"That's just it, I'm not sure."

"Sorry, can't help there, but I will tell you, don't follow the path deeper." Peter was a little puzzled by the advice and his expression showed it. The squirrel continued, "There is a cottage back that way. A very neat, clean, and pretty cottage, if you understand what I'm saying?"

"I'm not sure I do."

"If you want to stay alive, don't go near it. Haven't your parents warned you about witches?"

"Right," Peter said, pretending to agree.

The squirrel looked deep into the woods to a place where the path disappeared behind the trees. "And she's not old…"

* * *

Evening continued to pass, but the entire day had looked like twilight. Peter brought the wood back to the tree house where he stacked it on the pile organizing the pieces by size as Mr. Thorne had instructed. He looked out across the wheat field toward the wall of trees. The woods were dark, almost impenetrable, and Peter took comfort knowing that the first day of getting wood was over. The tree house stood behind him with light peeking from the lower windows and even though it wasn't home, it did look warm and inviting.

Just before nightfall, Peter ate with Mr. Thorne and Master Key at the small table in the kitchen. The meal consisted of hard bread and a vegetable stew made from over ripe squash and corn. Peter devoured all that he was given while Mr. Thorne explained to him the virtues of good craftsmanship. "I don't toss things together. That's why we keep everything locked. Witches come and steal the toys, the furniture, whatever they can get their greasy fingers on. They are expert thieves. Some of those pieces take me days to make and a lost chair can set me back a week."

Master Key listened for a while but seemed to know the speech all too well. His glance drifted to the small circular window just a few feet from the table. A cold wind was brewing outside, whipping leaves against the window panes.

"Winter's just around the corner," said Master Key with trepidation. The room was quiet for a moment. Peter couldn't tell if the comment was made with hope or dread. Oddly, it seemed a little of both.

"Any day, any day..." Master Key said as his voice trailed off a bit. Peter then sensed the dread. It wasn't that winter was so bad, rather, it was as though Master Key had said this before but again and again with less excitement until the whole business became uncertain. Mr. Thorne settled back in his chair, belly full. Peter continued to eat, still looking a little bewildered, lost, and homesick.

"In a few weeks, we'll pack the cart with all the goods for the sale at the Square Market." Mr. Thorne said.

"Is that a town?" Peter asked as he pulled the spoon from his wooden dish.

"No, it's a marketplace in the Square. It comes once a year, in a great walled city beyond the forest."

"Amberville," said Master Key with a grin as though the thought of it made him happy.

"A zestful place where people from all over the world bring their finest crafts and wares for sale in the Square. It's what we've worked for all year. A time and a place to show one's best work," Mr. Thorne added.

"Maybe you are from Amberville," said Master Key.

Peter shook his head. "It doesn't sound familiar."

Mr. Thorne continued to eat. "After the market, you can go to Port Is-A-Bell, beyond Amberville, a few days. They have ships from all over the world. I'm sure you can find your way home from there."

Peter said the words slowly "Port Is-A-Bell."

"The ships travel to far off lands...other cities and towns, faerie islands," continued Mr. Thorne.

"Can we go?" Master Key asked.

"No," answered Mr. Thorne abruptly as he dabbed his whiskers with a cloth napkin.

"You carve each one?" Peter pointed to the furniture and toys in the workshop.

"Hmph. Carve. What? Like meat or cheese?" Mr. Thorne dropped his napkin onto the table. "It's sculpture. It's art. It takes years to learn skill and craft but most importantly it takes vision, imagination." Mr. Thorne rose from his chair and carried a lantern from the kitchen into the workshop. A sphere of warm light pushed deeper into the tree illuminating the unfinished work.

"You can't make something unless you see it first."

"What do you mean?" Peter asked.

Mr. Thorne held a small block of wood in his hand. "Look at this. What do you see?"

"A piece of wood," Peter said.

"A piece of wood. And this?" Mr. Thorne held up a miniature wooden horse.

"A horse."

"This is a horse but so is this," Mr. Thorne raised the block of wood, "Do you see the horse?"

Peter, still unsure, shook his head that he didn't.

"It's inside. The key?" Mr. Thorne raised his finger, "Imagination."

"I don't see it. How?"

Mr. Thorne took a knife and peeled a corner off the block. "That's not a horse." He then pulled another shaving from the block, letting it fall to the floor, "That's not a horse." Peter's expression grew softer at the light humor.

"You see, every chair, every nightstand, every rocking horse has a home," Mr. Thorne said as he illuminated a nearly finished horse with the golden glow from the lantern. "Each piece is made for someone. I don't know who, but sometimes I try to imagine them when I'm working. I can see them as I plane the surface and sand the rough spots. The person who comes to the display and stares transfixed at this horse, thinking it was specially made for their son or daughter. The look that says this is the piece they had been looking for all along. It is the one." Mr. Thorne's familiar stern expression gave way to a warmer look, a look of deep satisfaction. "Every piece here has a home, and every home can be found in Amberville."

CHAPTER FIVE

NIBBLE, NIBBLE…

The evening was late. Peter was very tired and he could only think of sleep. He lumbered up the circular stairs and went to his small room on the second floor of the tree house. There was a round window a few feet from the bed that he locked and checked several times. Though no one mentioned anything about witches at dinner, Peter felt uneasy and remembered that flying monkeys could still be nearby. However, he found that his fear of monkeys had waned and he even thought for a brief moment that maybe he wished his kidnappers would come back for him. Maybe they would take him somewhere else. Perhaps home. He pulled at the window one last time with a firm hand

and decided that all was secure.

Peter took off his over clothes and pulled the covers down on the ornately fashioned bed, complete with pumpkins and corn carved into the headboard. Even the bedpost knobs were shaped like small pumpkins with a light garnish of leaf and stem to add a touch of intricacy. Peter sat on the edge of the bed with a small piece of paper and a crude ink pen. He thoughtfully sketched a simple outline of his old house with only a lantern for light. He put pen to paper and paused as though adding any more details was impossible. Peter crawled into bed, looking lost in imagination and failed by memory. The covers were cold, but with some wiggling about, he quickly warmed and fell asleep with only a few breaths.

Outside the wind stirred—another chilly night of autumn. A few hours later, a shadow pushed across his bed. The moonlight from the window was being blocked by something.

The witch was young and strong enough to climb. She gripped the side of the tree firmly with her long tenuous fingers. Her elongated facial features moved parallel to the windowpane. With a protruding right eye, she scanned the inside of the room. Her movements were controlled and animal-like. Her eyes, white with a small dark gray pupil in the center, strained to take in the image of the form under the covers of the bed. She smelled the cracks of the windows and sensed Peter inside.

After a few moments, she descended off of the tree and began her routine of looking for things to take, tools, toys, items left outside. She checked locks and overturned cans. The clatter woke Peter. He opened his eyes and heard the commotion coming from the yard.

The witch crawled underneath the window of the small cottage next to one of the sheds. However, Master Key slept peacefully inside, wearing his earmuffs, oblivious to the noises.

Peter pulled the covers down so that he could check to make sure his window was closed and that there was no one in the room with him. He appeared to be alone, safe. Cautiously, he moved the covers back, enough to pull his legs over and get out of bed. When Peter got to the window, he kept low and slowly raised his head to peer down into the yard. He heard another *bang* coming from the back near the woodpile. The shadow of something moving under the moon's light swept across the yard. The fluctuating lines of darkness came from something that moved like nothing Peter had ever seen. He didn't breathe, just stared motionless at the strange glimpses he couldn't comprehend.

Like a child smelling sweets, the witch sensed the boy was watching and she scampered back to her sack. With hungry eager movements, she lowered her bird-like head into the dirty old bag and reached in to extract a shiny red ball.

It rolled gracefully over the indentations of the yard and then stopped near the base of the tree. Peter looked at the ball intently then looked back to where it came from—the black void beyond the woodpile. There was something out there. He stared directly at the void and at the witch even though he could not see her.

The witch hunched down close to the ground and stared back at him. Her cloudy white eyes strained at the image. She began to breathe heavily as she realized that the boy was watching her instead of eyeing the prize, the lure.

Peter checked the lock on the window again and then returned to bed. However, this time, he kept his head above the rim of the covers staring at the window.

* * *

Frost was on the pumpkin the next morning, just as it was the day before. The eerie light of morning came just like the eerie light of dusk. Before anyone else was awake, Mr. Thorne started early only to discover that his saw was missing. After he railed at Master Key for a few minutes for not counting all the tools before locking them up, Mr. Thorne went back into the workshop to finish the legs of a chair.

At first, Peter just listened to all the sounds coming from outside. The morning was cold and he kept perfectly still under the heavy blankets. Then, a strange feeling came over him. He remembered getting up the night before and looking out the window. He thought about it but couldn't figure out whether the experience was a dream or not. It seemed part of his memory, but the concrete details of it were fleeting, vague, and without much coherence. The agitation within him quickly dispelled the notions of cold, and Peter knew it was time to get up and begin his chores. At least it would be something to take his mind off the night's strange and uncomfortable confusion.

He walked tiredly downstairs and pulled off a small block of bread from the main loaf and held it in his mouth while he tied the laces on his black leather shoes. Mr. Thorne looked up from his work. "Two trips today Peter. I need more wood. Much more."

Peter nodded and buttoned his wool coat as he walked out the door to find Master Key.

"Keys?"

Master Key was just outside the ragged old fence that lined the side of the tree house.

"Bad news. Very bad," Master Key said while he scratched his temple and fumbled through his keys as though they held the answer.

"I know. The saw."

"A witch, right here in the yard." Master Key shivered as though the very words made him cold. As Master Key talked about what had happened, Peter again remembered going to the window. He recalled peering down to the place next to the woodpile and hearing the strange sounds.

"Is that why you wear those?" Peter asked, indicating the red earmuffs.

"They make terrible sounds Peter. Sometimes they talk in beautiful voices to trick you. I've heard them. Like a mother calling you for dinner, having you for dinner."

Master Key clenched his keys tightly. "Did you see her?"

"I don't think so," Peter answered.

Master Key was gravely serious. "Still don't believe in witches?"

"I don't know what was in the yard last night. Maybe it was a raccoon. Maybe it was—"

Suddenly, Peter remembered the red ball. He glanced over to the spot it was left resting last night but there was nothing there.

"—Did you find a red ball this morning?" he asked with urgency.

"A red ball...no," said Master Key as he gave a cursory glance over the yard.

"There was a red ball right over...in front of the door, last night. It rolled up from," Peter pointed beyond the wood pile, "back there."

Master Key's eyes grew wide and he grabbed Peter's arm firmly. "That's very bad Peter. I think a witch knows you're here."

"What?" Peter asked as he pulled away.

"She's hunting. If I were you, I would be very careful. Extremely careful." Master Key looked as though standing next to Peter was implicating him in the danger. He was visibly nervous and fearful.

Mr. Thorne leaned out the door. "I don't give room and board to talkers. Let's go. Chop, chop!"

"Will you go with me today?" Peter asked.

"I'm sorry, but no thank you," said Master Key shaking his head.

"Then will you walk with me to edge of the field?"

"What for?" asked Master Key warily.

"Tell me everything you know about witches."

Master Key turned a shoulder to him. "But you don't believe in them."

"Will you tell me?"

Peter and Master Key walked over the small ups and downs of the dusty dirt path that cut through the wheat. As they approached, Peter looked at the woods with even greater fear than he had before. He didn't tell Master Key, but he knew that something was in the yard last night and it wasn't a raccoon. The gears of Peter's imagination were once again starting to turn. They weren't turning so much that Peter was vividly picturing witches but just enough to where an ominous feeling was creeping over him.

"They live in the forest?" Peter asked.

"It's not just any forest. It's Three Tree Wood," said Master Key.

"My mind has played plenty of tricks on me lately, but even I know there are more than three trees out there."

"Of course, but the forest grew from just three trees, although it should've been four."

"I don't understand," Peter said.

"A long time ago, there were four sisters," Master Key began. "They lost their parents when they were young and they lived on their own in a small cottage. They grew old together and they always took care of one another. After each one died, the other sisters planted a tree over her grave. This happened until there was only one sister left. But when she died, there was no one to plant a tree in her honor. Some say she died of natural causes, others say it was a witch who killed her. Either way, Three Tree Wood is cursed."

"What about the trees? Where are they?"

"I've never seen them, but I have heard they are deep in the heart of the forest. If the trees are still living, they are the oldest. You know, come to think of it, I'd really prefer not talk about witches too much."

"Ever since I've been here, it's all witches, all the

time. You can't stop now."

"Alright. Alright," Master Key paused, "Let's see, they eat children."

"Just children or anything short?"

"I don't know and I don't want to find out. Are you going to listen? Are you going to take this seriously? Remember, you asked me." Master Key was not amused by the question. Peter didn't respond; there would be no more remarks like that. Master Key regained his focus and started again.

"They come out in fall and feed until winter, and then they go into hiding, mostly dark caves deep in the forest." Master Key furrowed his brow trying to remember other details. "They are made of acid, oil, and bile. All stomach, all hunger so their skin is greasy and they leave a mark on things they touch. When they are young, they are very fast and strong but when they get old, they lose their strength and usually stay away from people. But don't be fooled, an old witch is very tricky and clever. The worst though is a young witch. I saw one once when I was out cutting wood. She was holding onto the side of tree watching me."

Master Key made his hands into gripping claws. He then bulged his eyes and lowered his brow, sinister like. His voice was lower and darker.

"She looked like a stone. Not a single movement, except her mouth. It trembled a little."

"What did you do?" Peter was pulled into the story.

"I ran, as fast as my little legs could take me. A young witch can run and climb like a spider and I hate spiders. Although I hate them less than witches. Hmm, spiders."

It was as though Master Key was recalling another event letting his own imagination or memory run away from him. "What was I talking about? Spiders? No. Witches. Young witches. A young witch isn't afraid of anyone or anything. If a window is left open, she will snatch a child from their bed."

Though fearful to hear another chilling detail, Peter thought of a question about the previous night's disturbance in the yard. "What about the red ball?" he asked.

"The red ball?"

"The red ball, in the yard last night."

"Oh yes," Master Key said regaining his train of thought. "A witch lure. Most will use toys or trinkets to draw a child closer to their traps and their houses are lures too. If you ever find a house in the woods that looks inviting, stay away." Master Key's voice finished haunting-like.

"Is that all?"

"Old witch, young witch, small witch...hmm...I don't think there is anything else. I'm sorry Peter, you look pale. Try not to worry."

"Sure," Peter answered without much confidence as he turned to enter the forest. As he left the relative safety of the open field, Master Key called out, "Good luck Peter. Don't get eaten!"

Peter trudged off into the woods with his hatchet and cart once more. He made fast work of cutting the wood into the proper sizes and sat for a moment on one of the small stumps. The ever-present rustling of leaves was the only sound until a blackbird jumped from tree to tree. Peter watched it swoop down to the ground, scavenge for a seed, and then alight to the safety of a branch. The blackbird flew over him and disappeared into the forest.

Peter remembered the squirrel he encountered so he decided to walk a little deeper to see if his acorn throwing friend was home. After a few taps to the trunk, Peter waited for a response. Nothing. He climbed up a few feet and peered into the hole. No squirrel. Only a covering of acorns filled the bottom.

He then remembered what the squirrel told him about the house that was deeper inside the woods. For the first time, Peter became very curious about this information. He imagined a house with a mean old lady but nothing close to what Master Key had told him about witches. With hatchet in hand, Peter decided to walk the path.

After some distance, Peter detected smoke in the air. The first sign that the squirrel was telling the truth. A little farther and the smoke became more prevalent. Peter could see a small house just a little ways off the path. The forest was so gray and brown but this little cottage stood out with all its color. The walls were yellow and blue. The trim was red and the steps were orange. Peter peered around a tree and looked carefully at every detail. He remembered everything Master Key and the squirrel told him, but he wanted so badly to get closer to this aberration. He wanted to get to the bottom of all the talk that had passed and this peculiar cottage held the truth.

Peter scanned behind him and to both sides before he moved to the next tree. He kept getting closer to the cottage until finally there weren't any more trees to hide behind to get a better view. He was either going to investigate or turn back. The place looked harmless, he thought. Nothing that grotesque could live there.

With a deep breath, he stepped away from the safety of the tree trunk and walked out into the small open area in front of the cottage. He stepped over a few patches of muddy ground but did not notice the elongated four-toed print set next to where his last footing was. Maybe if he had, he would've turned back.

Peter hit the first step and looked one more time behind him. The woods were all clear and he did not believe he was being followed so he continued up to the door, which was nearly all the way open. From where he was standing, he could see a living room with wooden chairs. He thought to himself that some of the furniture looked very similar to the pieces made by Mr. Thorne. The room was very clean and there was a fireplace on the back wall although the flame was almost out.

A monster does not keep such a place, Peter told himself as he pulled his hand into a fist. He tapped twice on the side of the doorway. No one answered. Cautiously, he stepped inside. There was a strange smell. Peter instinctively raised his hatchet a few inches just to be ready for grandmother or monster. He would not take chances.

As he turned his head, he could see the beginnings of a kitchen to his left. He leaned over and stepped inside the divider to get a better view. There was a long cutting island down the center. Large pots and pans hung from the ceiling and were set on the far wall. In the corner, there was a hulking stove. More utensils dangled from the ceiling—heavy knives and other sharp devices. Then, Peter saw them.

In the very corner of the kitchen, there were four greasy metal cages, each three feet high, suspended from the heavy wooden rafters. His heart stopped, when from inside the fourth cage, a dirty white shape moved inside and the sullied face of a young girl was staring directly at him.

There was a moment of silence. The girl's face was wet with tears. Her eyes were red. She said something to Peter but it was so low that he could not hear it. He moved closer as she continued to say the same thing over and over. Finally, he heard the words.

"She's hungry. She's hungry. She's hungry…"

The girl looked down at a large shallow pot set next to the stove. Peter swallowed hard and peered into the pot, half covered by a dirty rag. The strange smell came from there and he pulled back.

"Ate him first," she whispered hoarsely as she gripped the dirty metal bars of her cage. Peter took a deep breath and jumped up onto the center island and put his face up to the girl. He grabbed onto the heavy padlock.

"Where's the key?" Peter asked urgently as he put his hands on the metal rods. The girl shook her head that she didn't know and then touched his hand with her own.

"Go. Get out before she comes back," she begged.

"No." Peter tilted his head.

"Don't stay. She's coming back." Peter had never heard anything like what she was saying. Not just the words, but the expression. It was a look of intense sadness and it felt as though he had fallen into a deep well holding on to her.

Peter looked down at his hatchet. "Lean back." He swung hard but the padlock stayed firmly locked as the cage wavered back and forth hitting the others.

The girl's eyes locked and fixated on something behind Peter. He knew what it was. Quickly, he spun around, looking straight out the front door—logs fell, as though from midair, onto the floor and porch. Two rolled inside and the others rolled back down the steps. He exhaled in shudders and saw something drip onto the end of the wooden island. At first the liquid looked like water. The marks got closer. It wasn't water—it was oil. Peter looked up at the ceiling above him.

The contorted shape of a witch gripped the rafters tightly as she moved toward him. Her eyes glared down at him as though she was trying to hypnotize him and her voice was beautiful and soothing. "Be still little one. I won't hurt you."

For a second, Peter was motionless, almost hypnotized by the wretched figure. He saw her long arms begin to sweep around him. She opened her mouth and her rancid breath, saturated with the stench of rotten meat, dropped onto him.

The trance was broken. Peter dove under her and rolled out from the front side of the cutting island. He ran for the front door but it slammed shut and locked. The witch dropped onto the table, turned, and scampered toward him just as he pulled to the side and ran into the living room. Peter went to another door and opened it. Looking up, he found a closet full of toys and other wooden trinkets stacked to the top of the ceiling.

The witch pushed off the front door and sprang toward Peter once more. He pulled the pile of wooden toys over causing them to tumble onto the advancing witch. Peter backed away from the closet into the living room again and could see that the witch was only temporarily impaired. He frantically searched the room for some way out and stopped looking when he saw the fireplace. Without a second thought, Peter crawled into the fireplace and started upward through the chimney.

The witch threw the last chair and toy soldier off of her body and crawled cautiously into the living room. She dropped low and smelled the floor rubbing her long contorted nose against the wood. With each snort, puffs of dust blew up from the cracks in the wood.

Peter got to the top of the chimney and put his hand on a loose stone. At first, he pulled his hand away from it, but then thought of an idea. Peter placed his free hand back onto the stone and dislodged it. It was a risky plan, but he didn't have time to doubt it. After a deep breath, he let go, and dropped the stone down the chimney.

It hit the bottom grate with a loud *clang*. The craning head of the witch immediately snapped in the direction of the fireplace. Her thin lumpy body wrenched under her oily dress with every stride toward the fireplace opening.

Peter glanced down to find her angrily squealing at him but all her words were garbled from the liquid in her voice box. The witch crawled up the chimney just as Peter made his way out of the opening. He took a step back from top of the chimney and balanced his hatchet. The eager witch made no attempt to be cautious. She raised her ugly head out of the opening.

And it was over.

Her name was Hannah. She was cold but covered with the fill of a hungry witch who now ceased to exist in this world. The late evening found the survivors walking the path close together. Behind them, Peter dragged an oil-soaked bag.

"My brother and I were playing away from the path in the forest," she started. "Before we could find our way home, it was dark. A few days passed, and we couldn't find a way out. We could never find a beginning or end to the forest and we were so hungry and tired. One evening, we smelled something good coming from that little house." Hannah's story ended there; the rest would not be spoken.

"I thought everyone believed in witches. Didn't anyone warn you?" Peter asked.

"Our parents warned us, but I never believed."

"Where is your home?" Peter did not want to pursue the realm of belief any longer.

"Amberville," she said carefully as though it was the

only thing she longed to see.

"I've heard Mr. Thorne talk about that place. A town?"

Hannah raised her line of sight as though she could imagine seeing it just a little ways off. "A walled village. A small city beyond the forest. It chases the sun—always twilight and night."

"Then why couldn't you find it?" Peter was confused.

"How can you chase the sun when the forest hides it from you?"

"You look at the shadows." Peter pointed down to the ground but found, unexpectedly, that they cast no shadow.

"Shadows belong to the night and the moon, but chasing the moon will not take you home," Hannah said as though she was speaking from experience. Peter panicked inside as he looked up at the treetops to find an eerie light above them. He looked for its source but in every direction the subdued illumination was the same. Hannah knew he was afraid. She remembered her own discovery and understood. Before Peter could make sense of what defied sense, the girl reached down and searched for his hand and clutched it tightly. The voice of the forest answered their connection with the cold wind. It was as though the woods sensed a change coming but could not find the will to make the song find a new chorus.

"Don't be afraid. It only makes them hungrier," she whispered.

CHAPTER SIX

HARVEST MOON

Mr. Thorne searched the edge of the woods with lantern in hand. Peter was long overdue, and while Mr. Thorne would never admit it, he was worried. He stepped deeper into the woods and looked back to make certain he could still see the safety of the clearing. He held his lantern high and stared deep into the forest. "Master Key," he said in low voice craning his head to see around the next bend of the pathway. "Master Key? Is that you?" A long silence followed. Mr. Thorne was just about to return to the clearing when a faint glow grew out of the dark and began to weave in curved bobbing lines.

Master Key came running down the path as fast as

his legs would take him.

"What is it?" Mr. Thorne asked urgently thinking that Master Key was being pursued by something terrible. Mr. Thorne was just about to take off when Master Key slowed and panted, out of breath.

"He's not there."

"What about the cart?" Mr. Thorne asked.

Master Key, still breathing heavily, stopped, and raised a finger that he would answer momentarily. "The cart is full. He cut the wood but no Peter."

Mr. Thorne sighed. "You know what this means?"

"I'm going to have to cut the wood now?"

"He's run off," said Mr. Thorne squinting his eyes.

"Maybe he found his way home," replied Master Key.

"Well, where's the cart?"

"I started to bring it, but I heard something on the path so I—"

"—You left it?" Mr. Thorne asked.

"It's dark. I don't get wood in the dark. I don't go into the forest in the dark."

Mr. Thorne sent a sharp glance to Master Key when a low creaking emanated from the woods. It grew louder and soon the ghostly shape of two figures emerged from the trees.

It was Peter, with the cart, and Hannah following closely.

"It's Peter," said Master Key with a big smile.

"I thought you ran off," said Mr. Thorne.

"Are you alright?" Master Key asked. Peter nodded slowly. Mr. Thorne escorted them back to the yard and Master Key asked what had happened but Peter was silent. The last light of dusk was slipping behind the horizon when Peter stopped at the fence line and pulled the greasy bag out of the cart. He placed it on the ground right in front of Mr. Thorne who watched warily. Slowly, Peter opened the sack and the contorted witch head rolled onto the dirt.

Startled, Master Key jumped back nearly losing his balance. "A witch!"

"No. Not anymore," Peter said calmly.

"You're just supposed to cut wood...just wood!" exclaimed Master Key.

Peter introduced Hannah to them and told the story of what happened in the cottage. Mr. Thorne listened carefully while stroking his beard, then went into his tool shed. He came out with a tall wooden stake in hand. In the moonlight, they took lanterns out and Mr. Thorne planted the stake in the ground where the wheat field met the yard. Then, they secured the witch head on the tip. Mr. Thorne told everyone this would be a warning to all witches that they were in dangerous territory. The assertion made Peter nervous, but he didn't object.

Mr. Thorne moved closer to the witch head and touched the long greasy hair with his fingers as though he had never encountered a witch up close. "Horrid, wretched beast. Good work Master Peter. One less thief roaming the forest tonight," he said making it clear that he was only concerned about his work.

"Still don't believe in witches?" Master Key asked.

Peter didn't answer. The adrenaline from his experience was starting to wear off and Peter found himself wanting to touch the witch as if in confirmation. He raised his hand slowly and stretched his finger toward her protruding nose. Just inches away, he stopped, thinking that she might come to life. Looking into her still gray eyes, he remembered her voice and the smell of her breath in the kitchen of the cottage. He remembered her ferocious pursuit and the strike of his hatchet. His finger made contact, running down the bridge of her nose toward her nostril. The texture was cold and slick. She was real.

Peter thought about Master Key's question. Belief. Had he forgotten, that just hours before, he was telling himself that he didn't believe in such things? And yet, here was a witch, frozen and lifeless, but a true animal of the forest. Peter's heart jumped and he stepped back. He didn't have to imagine anything. Witches existed. They lived, breathed, and hunted. Peter stared into the eyes again, thinking back to the cottage, reliving the experience, searing every physical detail into his memory.

Peter then turned to Hannah. She looked lost and

frightened much like he did when he first arrived at the tree house but Peter didn't think about this. His mind raced to thoughts of the future, thinking about what must be done next.

"I want to take her to Amberville. Back to her parents," he said.

Mr. Thorne shook his head. "Not yet. We'll leave soon enough, but there's wood to be cut...things to be made." Mr. Thorne faced Peter abruptly. "I need you here," he said. "She can stay with us until then."

Peter felt the impatience welling up inside of him. He thought about arguing or even taking Hannah to Amberville by himself, but before he could decide, Master Key stepped toward Hannah. "You look cold. Come inside and let me fix you something to eat," he said. Master Key led her into the tree house leaving Peter outside. The air was stagnant. Mr. Thorne locked his tool shed and went inside.

Peter was alone and he walked along the fence line kicking at the dry dirt. Dusk draped over the land like the last glow of a burning ember. The wheat field sloped here and there as it made its way to the edge of the woods and the heads of wheat swayed gently back and forth whispering in the faint evening breeze. Peter looked over the landscape and could see a glow pushing up from beyond the forest. It was the moon. A big orange moon rising above the darkness into the evening sky. He stared at it for a long time but no longer remembered how he thought of it as a beacon guiding him home as he did on his first night. In fact, he didn't even notice that this moon was different than the one he saw on the first night. All of those thoughts were gone, vanished altogether or temporarily forgotten, as though covered over by piles of new memories.

Instead, he found himself thinking about being in the woods alone. His fear was present, but he was acutely aware that it wasn't an overwhelming fear. He had seen the terror and knew it first hand and somehow this lessened the intensity of his fear. Peter took the cart to the woodpile and started to stack the logs. It was night now and Peter could barely see the outline of the witch head a few yards away. It was still, suspended in the moonlight, and Peter felt something new. He felt more confident, almost emboldened.

Inside the kitchen, Master Key placed the pot of broth over the fire and turned his attention to the vegetables on the table. He made fast work of cutting up the turnips, radishes, and carrots while Hannah sat quietly on the other end of the table.

"Do you like potatoes?" Master Key asked.

Hannah nodded.

"So do I," he said as he cut the potatoes into cubes and then tossed everything into the broth. He reached into a bowl for a pinch of salt then stirred the mixture as a light froth bubbled from the top and a savory smell began to waft through the kitchen.

"Mmm, delicious," Master Key said adding a little more salt. He climbed onto a stool and retrieved a bowl out of the cupboard. Carefully, he ladled some of the hot vegetable stew into the bowl and carried it to the table making sure not to spill any. He placed the bowl in front of Hannah then made a bowl of stew for himself and sat down.

Sitting with her hands on her lap, Hannah waited patiently. She was hungry but so much had happened that day that she felt worried and numb all at the same time.

Master Key took a bite then noticed that Hannah wasn't eating. He put his spoon down. "You're safe now," he said.

Hannah nodded again.

"You should eat something. It's good. It'll warm your insides."

"Where's Peter?" she asked.

"Here," Peter said as he came in from outside.

"Stew's on the stove. Help yourself," said Master Key.

"Thanks. Smells good Keys." Peter filled his bowl and sat down with Master Key and Hannah. They both noticed that Hannah hadn't touched her food.

"Still not hungry?" asked Master Key.

Hannah smiled and dipped her spoon in. She blew over it a few times and took a bite.

"It is good. Thank you," she said to Master Key.

The inhabitants of the tree nestled in for another night. In the quiet of the dark, Master Key removed his earmuffs. There were no more sounds coming from the yard, only the few remaining chirps of the season's last crickets. Master Key fell asleep listening to the rhythmic sounds of fall.

Up in the tree, Peter rested with eyes open. He thought about this world and tried to compare it to the things he remembered about his old world, but even the old images he held onto were fading. He tried to think of this world as a big dream but with every passing day, it became more real. He thought about himself somewhere in another room dreaming this world, but nothing seemed to help him leave this place. He knew he belonged somewhere else, but he still wasn't sure where. Maybe this wasn't a dream. Maybe he should let go of trying to wake from it and instead try to find a path home. If it was a place with a way in, there must be a way out.

Hannah rested closely with one arm draped over Peter's chest. He had delivered her from a dark fate and she felt safer next to him. Peter knew little about her, but he did not push her away. In some way, Hannah seemed familiar to him. He was at ease with her. He couldn't figure out how or why but wondered if maybe they shared a connection in the great walled city of Amberville. They were both strangers here and though he would never disclose it, he wanted her close. Without thought, without trying, Peter closed his eyes and fell asleep.

* * *

The darkness of sleep opened up and gave way to a familiar scene. The dark blue witch-like figure continued to search. Her name was Scardamalia and she seemed to float under the power of her spindly legs, where her small army of flying monkeys kept close. She was searching for what she had lost but the unchanging time was working against her.

Peter followed her and the small encircling band of monkeys from a safe distance. He knew he had seen her before and wondered who she was, what she was doing, and who she was searching for. Peter clutched the side of a tree and peered stealthily in the direction of the ethereal figure. He couldn't take his eyes off her. Her movements were like the mist, a gentle and fluid motion. She sensed his presence and slowly turned. Peter wanted to run and escape, but he couldn't move.

"Peter?" she said in an old voice. Peter shook and trembled with fear.

"No Peter, don't be afraid," she said to him trying to reassure him, trying to teach him. Peter could see that his skin was prickled with goosebumps; he was cold and chilled to the bone. "Don't be afraid. They can smell it." Scardamalia raised her arms, pulled long spindly fingers, and looked toward Peter who seemed completely immovable.

"Fall. A time that is neither dead nor alive," she started. "It is a pause where two worlds touch momentarily like that brief moment when waking from sleep where the dream world and the real world brush lightly, whispering to each other a belly of truths and lies."

Suddenly, there was another sound. There was something in the forest. It was all around him.

From the hollow of the tree house, Hannah called out, "Mr. Thorne." She came out of the room and entered the staircase chamber. "Mr. Thorne," she said again. From upstairs, there was a low grumbling sound, then a lantern glow pushed out of Mr. Thorne's room from the third floor. "Who calls?"

"Look, it's Peter..." Hannah pointed down to the last few stairs. Peter was holding onto the railing, moving his head side to side, sleepily.

"What's he doing up at this hour?" asked Mr. Thorne.

"He walks, but he's not awake. He's asleep," Hannah said.

"What?" Mr. Thorne came down a few steps holding his lantern in front of him.

"I've tried to wake him but—" Hannah continued but Mr. Thorne immediately understood and hurried down to the second floor. "—No, no, don't. He's sleepwalking. We mustn't wake him."

The sounds around Peter grew louder. There was a rustling in the fallen branches and leaves. There were voices calling after him...witches. Peter could see the lumpy huddled masses emerging from the gray of forest. Their faces were concealed under the cloak of their hoods, but their bent noses thrust out, jutting up and down as though they were smelling their way to Peter. The witches were everywhere, closing in on him but he still could not move. He was completely immobilized with fear. He glanced up again to the path but Scardamalia was no longer there.

Hannah looked to Mr. Thorne, "Why can't we wake him?"

"If a sleepwalker is shaken from their dream, they will be pulled from their walk in an untimely and disturbing manner. If you were to wake Peter now, he would be so shaken from his awareness of his sleepwalking, he might not be able to sleep again. It's better to lead him back to bed and hope that he stays there."

"Are you certain?" Hannah questioned.

"Quite," said Mr. Thorne.

While Mr. Thorne and Hannah were still discussing the matter, Peter moved off of the staircase down into the kitchen.

"Peter?" Hannah discovered he was gone. Mr.

Thorne brushed by her with the lantern and pushed the light down to the first floor. "This way..."

Peter staggered toward the front door. He was just about to open it when the shriek and chatter of flying monkeys pelted the front door window. Peter immediately woke and screamed out in horror. Mr. Thorne and Hannah slammed the door shut. The monkeys were gone.

CHAPTER SEVEN

PETER, PETER, PUMPKIN EATER

Days passed but fall remained. Peter, who had once reveled in the season of adventure and mystery, grew tired of the leaves, the chilly evenings, and the hint of a winter that never came.

It was a few days later, or so he thought. Peter had just pulled another cart full of wood back from the forest. He stacked it neatly on the pile and pulled the tarp back over it to protect it. That's what Peter told himself, but as soon as the idea was in his mind a question had arisen—protect it from what? He had been here some time, even though he couldn't say exactly how long. Maybe he should have marked the days to keep track, but no matter, fall was clearly seen in the color of the trees and the chill in the weather. However, something was missing. Rain, he thought. That's why he put the tarp over the wood, to protect it from rain. However, there had been no rain or at least no rain that he could remember.

When he parked the cart on the side of the yard, he saw something moving in the branches in the first row of trees. Something had just alighted, something had just chattered. He remembered the sounds of the flying monkeys and stopped to watch and listen but no further sound or sight came. There was nothing but the small wavering of a branch where something had been perched moments before. A few yards to the right, a pair of crows came up from above the branches and stole Peter's glance and then his vision drifted off to the seemingly close horizon again. Another storm was threatening, but one look and kick of the ground with his shoe immediately told the tale that everything was still very dry. The look of a storm was just that, a hollow threat.

He went inside the tree house for a little while. His loud footsteps could be heard clambering up the staircase, then returning down to the first level. Peter emerged from the front door, quicker. He was looking for something or someone.

Inside Master Key's house, the small man examined a lock that looked decayed. The heavy metal device was rusted and its outer shell had been stripped of its seal. Peter stepped onto the small raised platform in front of the door with the lower half of his body blocking the short doorway.

"Keys?" Peter stooped down and peered in. "Where's—?" Peter spied the damaged lock. "—What happened?" he asked.

"Witch lick."

"Witch lick?" Peter forgot his original question and was mesmerized by the marred lock sitting on Master Key's workbench. "Luckily, I don't think the bile got inside," Master Key said as he used a flat blade to scrape off some of the corrosion.

"How does that happen?" Peter said as he projected a finger to examine it.

"Don't touch it! There's still stomach acid there. Digestive juices. Very potent."

Master Key used a pair of crude tongs to pick it up and dip it into a bucket of baking powder. The surface of the casing bubbled as the acid was neutralized.

"And we'll let that soak for a while."

"You forgot to tell me about this," said Peter.

"That's probably because I've never seen it before." Master Key wiped his hands on an old rag.

"Then how do you know it was a witch?"

Master Key stared at Peter with a look of bored disbelief.

"It stinks like a witch. Her prints were all over the yard, around the doors, windows, everything."

"What did she do?" Peter asked peering into the bucket.

"By the looks of it, she licked it. I think she licked the doors too. Very bold Peter, very bold. I've never seen anything like this before. It has to be a young one, a real hungry witch."

Peter pulled back and checked the front of the door where he found dark stains on the wood near the latches and locks. "If we're lucky, maybe she got splinters in her tongue."

"This isn't funny. It's bad. Very bad." Master Key had the shivers again. The whole experience unnerved him. He was dealing with something he had never encountered before and it took any safety he felt residing at the tree house and chased it off.

"Are you okay?" Peter asked, looking concerned.

"I don't like it Peter. I've never seen witches so bad. It's the worst season yet. It's not normal."

"Don't worry, it'll be all right. Remember, winter's almost here and they'll hibernate soon…" Peter trailed off on the last part, as though the assertion troubled him.

"Where's Hannah?"

"Last time I saw her she was at the edge of the field. I warned her to stay out of the forest," said Master Key.

Before Master Key could add anymore, Peter bolted out of the door, through the dirt yard, and onto the path. When he arrived at the dividing line between the field and the forest, no girl could be found. Peter spun around and called for her.

"Hannah?"

No answer returned, but there was only one way to go...into the woods. It was easy for Peter to say a few confident words a few moments before to Master Key, but seeing that Hannah might be in the forest alone, all confidence and courage had left him.

Peter swallowed hard then took his first step. He followed the path to the small clearing of felled trees and there he spied Hannah sitting by herself on a stump. Her head was low. Leaves tumbled end over end between them. Peter could hear her crying softly. She seemed to know he was standing behind her.

"I'm sorry. I shouldn't have left like that."

"Are you hurt?"

"No."

"Sad?"

"I thought it would be safe. I came here to let it all out because I couldn't before. No matter how much I wanted to cry, I couldn't. The tears wouldn't come." Hannah wiped the remaining tears on her sleeve. She looked up, trying to pull any new ones back.

"Now, it won't stop."

"Is there anything I can do?"

"A brother. You can't bring them back. You can't help. Nothing can be done." Hannah lowered her head into her hands. Peter felt awkward, not knowing what to do or say. She looked up again, eyes red. "I miss him. What I would give to see him again. Talk to him." She was finally able to say it and that brought more tears. She sniffed, still fighting the feelings that threatened to take over. For Hannah, it was not fear that imprisoned her, it was grief. She looked at Peter as though she wanted him to see what she fought so hard not to show anyone else then she wiped the tears again with her sleeve and looked away.

Peter went to her side and placed his hand gently on her shoulder. In a peculiar moment of time, the cold air parted and there was a touch of warmth between them. The forest didn't seem quite so dark and Peter and Hannah didn't feel quite so alone. For every day that seemed the same, this moment was like a new page entering the world with the dance of leaves that tossed and turned every second, every minute.

"We should get back. It's getting dark." Peter looked around the clearing. It was quiet. Hannah stood up and faced Peter.

"Are you afraid…of the dark?" Hannah asked.

"No," he said quickly.

"All kinds of strange things out tonight." She glanced up at the branches. "I'm sure of it."

Peter's mind latched onto what she said. He felt it as she spoke the words. Words that felt familiar as though he would be able to predict the next one. And then he said, almost automatically, "Out here, it's just like any other night."

The sensation intensified. It was that feeling of recognition and familiarity, like seeing yourself as an actor playing out a part in a scene, a part that you had played before, and you knew it. Peter's expression darkened.

"Has something happened?" Hannah asked. Finally, the cold air came and the chill of fear swept around them both. Peter remembered the locks back at the tree house and knew once again that the feeling of safety was fleeting.

"Come on," Peter said gently, giving Hannah his hand. Hannah accepted it but immediately knew that Peter was very afraid. He was thinking of witches, and she could feel the tiny goosebumps on his skin. She stopped him and looked down at his wrist.

"Just a little cold, that's all," he said.

"No Peter, listen very carefully. They are the marks of fear, and witches can sense them. Remember what I told you. Do not be afraid. Don't think on it."

"I know, but it's too late. Come on."

They ran over the clearing back onto the path as the whirl of wind chased their heels out of the forest.

Peter and Hannah returned to the tree house to find Master Key standing near the back next to the wooden stake that once carried the head of a slain witch.

"Mr. Thorne!" he yelled just as he saw Peter and

Hannah coming over the last rise in the path. "Come quick!"

Mr. Thorne looked down at Master Key puzzled. All that was left was the stake, pushed over a little in the dry crumpled ground.

"What did you do?"

"Nothing," Master Key said.

Peter too wondered, "What happened?"

"There were two of them." Master Key pointed down to the barely visible four-toed prints left in a patch of powdery dirt.

"They took it?" Peter asked.

"They must have. This morning I found one of my best chairs missing from the shed. I thought it was—" Mr. Thorne turned to Peter abruptly. "—You are going after them?"

Peter was taken a back. Hannah looked to Peter waiting for an answer. He couldn't tell if she wanted him to go or stay. Peter swallowed, "Now?"

"Yes, they can't be far," Mr. Thorne said.

"Hunting two witches is dangerous. Too dangerous."

"Well, when? We leave for Amberville in a few days and there isn't much time to make up for lost work. I thought you were a witch hunter." Mr. Thorne walked away in frustration.

Peter scanned the yard, "Did they take anything else?"

"Well, I'll have to look," said Mr. Thorne.

"Then I don't see what's the big hurry." Peter shrugged his shoulders.

"They're witches. They'll keep coming if you don't stop them." Mr. Thorne spun around to face Peter. "You're a witch hunter. Hunt them," he said poking a finger into Peter's chest to emphasize the point.

"I'm not a—" Peter stopped mid-sentence and saw that Hannah was anxious to hear what he had to say. Could he let her down? Could he let any of them think that he was unable to help now? "—I'm not just a witch hunter. I…know how to keep them away."

Mr. Thorne threw up his hands.

"Who wants to keep them away?"

"We do," Peter said confidently.

"What about cutting off their heads?" asked Master Key.

"Only when it's necessary. If I kill another, more will come and that's not what we want. What we want is to keep them away for good."

"And how are you going to do that? We don't have any more witch heads," observed Mr. Thorne.

"Yes Peter, how are you going to keep witches away without a witch head?" asked Master Key.

"I have a plan." Peter paced a little. "To keep witches away requires—" He was stalling again for more time. He most certainly did not want to hunt another witch, not unless he absolutely had to. He remembered the last one all too closely. Her gray shiny skin covered in welts. Her strained animal eyes. Her teeth. Her breath. Then, he thought of something. From where, he wasn't sure, but an idea just appeared in his mind.

"—Pumpkins. Big ones. Master Key, where can we find a pumpkin patch?"

"Pumpkins?" Master Key asked.

"Yes. Isn't there a pumpkin patch?"

No one answered. They still were confused by the witch hunter's request and perhaps Mr. Thorne wasn't completely convinced of the plan. Peter sensed this and knew he had to work harder at selling the idea.

"Have you ever seen a witch with a pumpkin?"

The three shook their heads and made low *no* sounds under their breath. Peter secretly made a sigh of relief.

"Where I come from, we keep witches away with a pumpkin, one with two eyes and a mouth cut out."

"You cut the pumpkin?" asked Master Key.

"Yes, we cut the pumpkin. It's called a jack-o-lantern. You've never heard of this?" Peter waited to hear the answer, a little unsure of what they were going to say.

"No." Mr. Thorne lowered an eyebrow.

"Strange, very strange," said Master Key as he tugged on his ear pondering this creation.

"This works?" said Mr. Thorne.

"Yes. We put a candle inside and the pumpkin becomes a bright orange lantern. It scares away anything evil. Now, if you'll show me to the pumpkin patch, I can start immediately. You do have pumpkins, don't you?"

Mr. Thorne was the first to speak. "Master Key, take Master Peter to the pumpkin patch at once. I want a jack-o-lantern."

"Yes Mr. Thorne, right away."

Over the main path heading to the west, chasing the always setting sun, Peter, Hannah, and Master Key walked up a small incline to find a clearing below filled with pumpkins. The pumpkins were all sizes, from twelve inches all the way to several feet across. Peter was stunned. His jaw dropped a little at the sight of such enormity and his eyes stayed fixed on a beautifully round specimen that stood a full five feet tall.

Peter ran down the hillside of dank peat and moss and entered the great pumpkin patch. Hannah and Master Key caught up to him after he winded his way through the labyrinth to the prize.

"It's the biggest pumpkin I've ever seen! A great pumpkin." Peter placed a hand on its side. "I've never seen anything like it." He stretched his arms out, hugging it while putting his ear to the side as though he was listening for a sign of life. "Keys, we'll need the cart."

Silhouetted against a violent orange sky, the hunters returned to the tree house with a cart full of pumpkins. They stopped in the center of the yard and dumped their freight. All rolled blissfully about, even the five-foot pumpkin, that nearly toppled Master Key's cottage. With light slipping away, Peter taught everyone the art of the jack-o-lantern. The art of imagining the face that was already there. The carving of strange and frightening expressions that watched you as you worked.

"It's like Mr. Thorne said, imagination is the key. See the face first then carve the pumpkin until everyone can see it," Peter said. Mr. Thorne inserted his knife and cut a triangular eye. He smiled and pressed through to reveal the opening.

"Here, I want to give it a try," said Master Key. "Give me the little saw."

Mr. Thorne handed him a saw.

"Hey, this is the big saw. Fine, the tiny saw, where is it?"

Peter moved to Hannah who was making a set of jagged teeth.

"How does it look?" she asked.

"Very scary," said Peter.

After a few hours of hard work, the new students had all of the small pumpkins completed and lit. Peter then tackled the beast. Hannah grabbed two more metal lanterns from the tree house to give Peter more light for his work and Mr. Thorne brought the large wood saws to help with the cutting of the facial features.

After some thought and deliberation, Peter took his small hatchet and cut marks for the eyes and mouth. He then climbed up to the top and hacked the outline of the lid. With the top pulled out, Peter descended into the pumpkin.

After some time digging and cutting, he began tossing out large clumps of bitter squash with enthusiasm. Everyone was delighted by the kill and they continued to work by roasting the seeds on a large skillet they placed on a fire they had built in front of the tree house. After another hour, Peter tossed his hatchet out the right eye and crawled out of the mouth. The four carvers, splattered with juice, rolled the new "jack" to the back of the yard. Master Key placed one of the large lanterns inside and the task was complete.

Peter walked out into the wheat field to view the glowing jack-o-lanterns from a distance. The rest followed. They smiled at the luminous sight of ten twisted faces, grinning, scowling, and scaring the night away.

CHAPTER EIGHT

SOMETHING BIG, THIS WAY COMES

The next few days passed quickly and the witches stayed away. Peter and Master Key cut plenty of wood for fires, for cooking, and for all of Mr. Thorne's woodworking. The season stayed the same, but Mr. Thorne reminded everyone that it would soon be time for the trip to Amberville. His projects were almost finished and in a matter of days, they would load up all the toys and furniture into the cart for the market in Amberville. This news seemed to raise the spirits of everyone, especially Hannah who was very eager to see her parents. Master Key was excited too, if for no other reason than to break the monotony of daily life at the tree house. For Peter though, it was hard to tell just what he was happy about. He had become so involved in the lives of those around him that he seemed to forget that he too was looking forward to something.

One night, Peter went upstairs to his room, leaving the sound of laughter and lively talk about Amberville on the first floor. All had memories and shared experiences of the great walled city except Peter. He enjoyed hearing their stories, but it soon became apparent to him that he didn't belong. He doubted he was from Amberville and it was unlikely he was from any other town in this world. Peter listened a little longer then closed his door, quelling the sounds from below.

He went to his nightstand and opened his paper sketch, which was now worn and tattered. The image was the same. There were a few lines here and there to show the basic shape but there was little detail in between. Peter picked up a chunk of colored wax from his lantern and went to his bedroom window. Slowly, he sketched the outline of his old house onto his window. He tried to add details to the image on the glass but nothing new could be added. He sighed and folded the paper and placed it in his coat pocket. Just outside the window, a gust of wind came up and snatched a cluster of leaves. They flew over the yard, beyond the woodpile, the shed, and the field toward the forest.

Another day. The four inhabitants of the tree house had just finished their meal of pumpkin stew and pumpkin pie when a new sound from outside was nearly drowned out by all the chatter. From deep within the heart of Three Tree Wood, a terrible wind stirred through the naked branches up into the sky above. Heavy rain clouds pushed onto the canvas and were moving over the canopy toward the tree house.

Inside the kitchen, Master Key lifted the teapot and offered more to Hannah and Peter. Peter watched and listened to the tea splashing lightly into each cup until they were both full. Strangely, his ears picked up a similar sound that continued after the tea had been poured.

"It's raining," Peter said just as he looked up from his stew. He sprang from his chair and opened the front door. A strong wind blew inside. Mr. Thorne stood up with his napkin still tucked into his collar.

"That's nonsense, there were no storm clouds threatening this evening," he said.

Everyone went to the door. All could see that a dark wave was moving quickly their way.

Mr. Thorne pointed. "See, there's no rain, now close the door Master Peter. You're letting cold—"

Just as the rain pelted the woodpile, it hit Master Key's shed and then swept over the tree house with great force.

"—rain in!" Mr. Thorne shouted right before Peter

slammed the door shut. A curtain of rain swept over the dusty ground with driving intensity.

A little later, Peter and Hannah were glued to the kitchen window, watching and listening to the rainfall. Peter poured himself another cup of tea and offered more to Hannah. "No thank you," she said. Hannah tore off a piece of bread and glanced at the pumpkins piled inside the kitchen. "Do you ever get tired of pumpkin?"

Peter thought a moment. They had eaten a lot of pumpkin lately. In fact, they had pumpkin, in some form or another, every single day. "Not really," Peter said. "I like pumpkin."

In the adjoining woodshop, Mr. Thorne and Master Key, each holding a metal cooking pot, stood ready for the next leak. Master Key watched the floor intently for signs of falling water while Mr. Thorne stared open-mouthed at the dark cavernous ceiling. He heard something. A trickle of water perhaps.

"Blasted wet weather," he muttered to himself. He knew a vein of water had gotten inside and he was close, but he didn't know how close until a few big drops of water came down and hit him on the face.

"Blasted rain," he said.

Master Key felt water hitting the back of his coat so he turned around, knelt down, and carefully placed a pot directly under the new drip. Meanwhile, Mr. Thorne, still cursing the weather, positioned his own pot under his own leaky discovery.

Hannah went back to her seat and placed her small hand gently on the windowpane. She watched the drops of water run down, joining one another, gaining strength and speed, on their way to the bottom of the glass.

"Have you always lived here?" Hannah asked, still looking at the window.

"No."

"Then how did you get here?"

Peter smirked a little. "How?" He thought a moment, searching his memory for an answer. "I remember only a few things from the first night. I remember the forest. I walked for hours. I remember the first morning at the tree house. I was lost, looking for my home. Sometimes it seems like yesterday. Sometimes it seems like years ago."

"So the tree house wasn't always your home?" asked Hannah.

"It is, but I remember telling Mr. Thorne that I was trying to find my home. Not this one."

Hannah thought about this. She glanced back to the window but looked beyond the rain streaked glass toward the trees. "The forest can play tricks. We can lose ourselves in it. Lose our way. I should know."

"I've had a few dreams lately. A few nights ago, I dreamt I was in a different place. I can't remember much...only a house," Peter said. He reached into his coat and pulled the old sketch of his home, the one made on the first night. He unfolded it carefully and showed it to Hannah.

"This house. I made that on the first night, but I can't add anything to it. There's a witch I dream of too. Not every night, but many times. She's different than the rest. In the dream, she wants me to follow her."

When Hannah heard this, she became very serious. She touched Peter's arm and leaned in toward him. "Tricks Peter. Witches will lure with anything they have. Steal your dreams if they have to." Hannah looked back to the rain outside. "It's strange. Maybe winter will come after all."

"I'll believe it when I see some snow," Peter said.

"Snow...what is that?" Hannah asked as though she was surprised that she asked the question.

"It's cold...and white." Peter answered with little thought.

"Sounds strangely familiar. What do you do with it?"

"Snow is great fun...you...there are lots of things..." The skin on Peter's forehead crumpled. He was having difficulty remembering. "You throw it at each other...and..."

"Does it hurt?"

"I don't think so." Peter shook his head; all memory seemed to halt his ability to gather any more details. "Why can't I remember?" he said.

"What's the matter?" Hannah tried to understand.

"I did all sorts of things in the snow, but now I can't see any of it."

The two sat in silence listening to the rain. Peter watched Hannah and could see her thinking back. A lost stare that went beyond the rain drops on the window. He had never seen her do this before but immediately recognized the expression—the look of not thinking back to what you did just an hour before or the day before, but a memory of something distant, buried deep in the mind.

"What are you thinking about?" he asked. For a second or two, she didn't let her mind acknowledge the question but then she blinked and looked at Peter.

"What did you say?"

"What are you thinking about?"

"My parents," she said almost sadly.

Peter waited again for her to start, but he could tell she was trying to sort something out. The look was a telling sign of something she remembered but it didn't make sense. He knew that feeling all too well.

"Isn't that strange?"

"What is?" Peter asked.

"I think I had been lost in the forest before...with my brother. They found us," she said.

"Who?"

"My parents...they found us and took us in. I'm

not sure they are my real parents. Could that be true? Why had I forgotten? And why can't I remember anything before that?" Again, Hannah looked lost in vague memories.

Back in the woodshop, Master Key spied another drip a few feet away so he went to the kitchen to look for another pot. Suddenly, the old drip moved. Mr. Thorne noticing this, after the fact, saw that the leak was a foot from where the pot was set.

"Master Key, this is no good. You're missing the leak altogether." Mr. Thorne moved the pot so that it was, once again, centered under the drip. He got up and spied the second leak a few feet away so he snatched the pot from Master Key's hands as the little man came out of the kitchen.

"Incompetent," Mr. Thorne quipped as he returned to his task. Master Key, perplexed, shrugged off the comment. The first leak moved back to the original spot unbeknownst to them. Master Key noticed that the pot was off a good foot, so he moved it to catch the water.

A few feet away, Mr. Thorne strategically placed the new pot under the third drip and stepped back satisfied that the job was complete. Master Key then noticed that Mr. Thorne hadn't placed his first pot directly under the drip so he moved the pot. The drips moved again, and Mr. Thorne noticed again that the pot wasn't in the right place.

"Master Key! Put them right under the water, like this! See?"

"I did Mr. Thorne! I put it right under," Master Key fumed.

"You've done no such thing, they're a foot away!" Mr. Thorne countered.

And so, as the drips continued to move, Mr. Thorne and Master Key followed one another around the room fixing the supposed incompetence left by the other one.

"You had this one all the way over here! There's no water here!" Mr. Thorne shouted while pointing down at the watery mess on the floor.

"Well, I saw you move that one just a moment ago and it isn't catching anything!" Master Key yelled back, throwing his arms out.

"I didn't move that one!"

"You did too. I just saw you!"

"Well, you moved this one!"

"Which one? That one?"

"No, this one."

"This one?"

"No, that one!"

"That one?"

And so on...

A few hours later, the inside of the tree house had quieted some. The only sound in the dark house was that of the wind, the rain outside, and the light *drip*,

drip sound of water falling into large pots set around the first floor and stairwell. The tree house inhabitants tossed and turned in their beds, unable to sleep soundly, from the medley of noises. *Drip, howl, pitter, patter, drip, howl.*

* * *

The next morning, Mr. Thorne came downstairs scratching his unruly hair. He pulled his old frock coat snuggly onto his shoulders and looked over the first floor, where he found a damp disorder, a spattering of full pots, buckets, and bowls. He walked through the woodshop inspecting his goods, looking under each tarped item to make sure they hadn't been damaged. He sighed deeply and rubbed his short whiskers around his chin and neck. The room was a mess but the important things appeared to be safe and dry.

Mr. Thorne shuffled slowly into the kitchen. Before getting anything to eat, he went straight to the front door, undid the locks, and opened it. He stepped out onto the muddy ground, stretched his arms out, and blinked his eyes as he did every morning. The yard was a terrible muddy mess and parts of the picket fence were lying on their side. A few boards were scattered around the yard with mud and leaves interspersed chaotically into the mix. A tired, gloomy expression pulled on Mr. Thorne's usual somber countenance.

His glance went from the purplish amber horizon to the small patch of mud right in front of him. Mr. Thorne's expression changed abruptly again. His eyes grew wide. Directly in front of him, he could see a series of four-toed witch prints clearly visible in the mud. However, these prints were not like the ones they had seen before. Rather, they were nearly four feet long. The tracks circled the yard and tree house, finally trailing off into the field toward the trees.

"The Great Big Witch," Mr. Thorne uttered ghostly white.

CHAPTER NINE

AMBERVILLE

The tree house was now in a frenzy to close up. Such information was almost unbelievable but apparently was very real. Three Tree Wood carried many secrets. Flying monkeys and talking squirrels were only a few. A witch almost the size of a tree was more than Peter could imagine but foot prints bigger than Master Key couldn't lie.

"We have to be gone before nightfall!" Mr. Thorne yelled with an armful of supplies. "Well before nightfall if we want to have a chance," he said urgently.

Inside the kitchen, Hannah hurriedly placed jars and baskets of food into wooden crates. Peter and Master Key moved through the room with a chair in each hand.

Peter loaded the first chair up onto the cart and pushed it to the front. He shook his head at Master Key. "I asked you if that was all. You said, 'old witch, young witch, small witch' What happened to big witch? You left out something very big!"

"Don't talk, just work! We need to get on the road." Master Key was in a sober and foul mood or maybe he was just extremely frightened. However, Peter couldn't let the subject go. How could he? There were massive foot prints all around to remind him of the impending danger. "Look at the size of her feet. Shouldn't we stay inside the tree? Wouldn't it be safer?" Peter asked from up on the cart.

"No, it wouldn't be safer. She just came to look us over. She'll be back tonight to finish us off."

"She can't knock down the whole tree," Peter said. Master Key didn't reply but instead handed up the second chair to Peter.

"They say she doesn't move very fast, so if Mr. Thorne is right, maybe we can stay ahead of her on the path."

Peter jumped down from the cart, but he wasn't convinced that the plan would work. He had seen a witch before and she was as fast as a spider, just like Master Key described. Master Key then started back for the front door.

"I don't believe this!" Peter yelled after him.

Master Key threw his hands up, "Don't argue! Don't talk! Just work!"

Mr. Thorne came out of the door just as fast as Master Key entered.

"Stop talking and get the food crates from Hannah!" Mr. Thorne yelled.

Peter took a deep breath and went back into the kitchen. Hannah had just finished filling a crate and she pushed it to the edge of the table to make room for the next one. She looked up to find Peter shaking his head. "I've never seen them like this."

"The Great Big Witch." Hannah said in a low tone.

"I heard, I saw, and I don't like it much either but—"

"—The faster we get to Amberville the better Peter. It might be our last chance."

"We could defend ourselves just as well here."

"She's a very old witch." Hannah said as though there was more to this comment.

"And from her name, I suppose the biggest," he said sarcastically.

"Well, a witch that size doesn't get that big from eating squirrels. She ate more children than any living witch. Finally, she got old, and stayed away from people. If she's come out, she's either very hungry or very afraid."

"Of what?" Peter said.

"Maybe you should've said 'of who?'"

Hannah handed the crate of food to Peter and looked at him. He was afraid. She could see a line of small goosebumps on his arm.

"See why it's not such a good idea to talk about this now."

"I'm sorry. I forgot."

"No more talk of witches. Think of home, think of safety, think of Amberville."

It was only another five minutes and the inhabitants were gone. The tree house sat empty under the gray clouds above. All was still in the small clearing, but not so in the forest. The witches were converging. Some by path, some by tree, but all were creeping closer to the tree house.

* * *

Later that afternoon, Mr. Thorne, tired from walking, pulled the cart off the path a little ways into the first row of trees. They pulled a tarp over the top with two poles holding the corners up. A low fog covered the ground, and underneath the cart, Master Key and Mr. Thorne took a brief rest. Peter and Hannah were tired but too restless or nervous to stay in one place, so Hannah convinced Peter to take a walk with her.

They discovered a narrow trail running over a

hillside. When they came down the other side, they found the ground wet and covered with moss. Peter tried to steady himself but the trail was slick. When he lost his footing, he fell into Hannah and they slid down through some leaves. They tumbled down, end over end, and hit the bottom. Peter groaned as he looked up at the bare branches. "Ugh." Hannah grabbed his arm and said "Look." They found themselves next to a small cemetery marked by a decrepit iron fence.

"I think we should get back to the cart. We don't want to get lost," Peter said picking himself up. Hannah didn't say a word as she squeezed through one of the breaks in the iron fence. The grave markers were old. Some were broken, lying on their side. Most had inscriptions that were so weathered, it was very hard to make out the words. Peter reluctantly followed as Hannah walked between the old gravestones. "Ancestors," she said as she walked between each one. She stopped at one and read an inscription.

"The soul has made a journey but now only fragments remain. All that is left is a longing, a fear, a loss, and a small piece of heaven and hell." Hannah looked up to Peter. "Like lost dreams."

"Like what?" he said.

"Lost dreams. When you dream a dream and in the morning you wake and it's gone. You know that something happened. Something important. Something learned. You're left with strange feelings but that's all."

Peter glanced down; he knew what she was talking about.

"They leave us a handful of pictures of another time and place. They are a part of us, but we know little about them. Sort of like ancestors," said Hannah. She bent down and placed her hands and fingers on the grave marker. "All that's left is a marker."

Unbeknownst to them, a set of bony hands had just settled on the top of the rod iron fence. Someone was watching.

"Too many lost dreams. Every morning I wake thinking they are telling me something, showing me the way home," Peter said.

"Perhaps they are," a voice said from the fence. Peter and Hannah looked up startled. Before them, loomed the sweeping blue figure of Scardamalia. She was tall, with her wide brimmed hat concealing her face. Peter and Hannah pulled back, hearts pounding, trying to get to the break in the iron fence.

Scardamalia moved gracefully along the outside of the fence. "Very bright girl," she said. "Fall is such a short season, such a short time. An autumn lost is much like a dream lost. It is come and gone, too fast. If there was anything in it, we'd only know by that strange tormented feeling telling us something was there but now it is gone. In the end, all that is left is an empty place to remind us, haunt us."

"Stay back," Hannah warned as they slipped through the break. They took steps backward always keeping an eye on Scardamalia.

"Been looking for you. Ever since that first night. I can help," she said to Peter who seemed to want to listen. He lingered in front of the fence as Scardamalia continued to move closer.

"I've seen you before," Peter said.

"Yes."

"You held me prisoner," he said as though the words surprised him.

"That's good. You remember. But things aren't always as they appear. Not captive. I needed to find you. It was the only way."

"Come on Peter. Don't listen to her." Hannah could see that Peter was reluctant to flee. Something seemed to draw him.

Scardamalia stopped a few feet away and craned her head a little. "I need your help. We all do."

Hannah pulled on Peter again. "Lies," she said trying to break Peter's interest.

"Our world is changing because it won't change. That is why you are here," said Scardamalia.

"No. She's lying. Don't listen!" Sarah pulled harder this time and yelled "Peter!"

Just then, a flash of wings descended. A swarm of flying monkeys dove in, trying to catch hold of Peter. Their strong little hands gripped the top of his shirt but Hannah swung hard and knocked them back. Peter ducked and narrowly missed the clutching hand of another.

Hannah tugged hard on Peter's arm and forcibly pulled him into the safety of the trees. They turned and climbed up the trail with the monkeys still pursuing, still swooping in after them. One monkey shrieked as it jumped from a tree branch onto Peter's back. He spun and tried to shake it off, but the creature latched onto him. When Peter fell back, the creature rolled onto his chest and screamed. Peter yelled out again and batted the animal away. He pulled himself up and made it to the top of the hill. He looked back once and could see Scardamalia motionless at the edge of the cemetery.

The monkeys came in from above and attacked once more, flying in through the trees. Peter and Hannah dashed into the forest, picking up speed as they went. Hannah leapt over a fallen log, veered right, and broke into an all-out run. Peter followed closely and looked back—the monkeys were having difficulty navigating the low-lying limbs and soon they fell behind. The cries faded in the distance but Hannah and Peter kept running. When Hannah made it to the top of the next hill, she stopped to catch her breath. Peter stopped alongside and looked back. They were alone. "Come on. We should get back," she said still winded.

* * *

The following day, the party made it to the edge of Three Tree Wood. As they passed the last line of trees, the group could see a small valley below holding the city of Amberville. At the sight of their destination, Master Key smiled. "We made it."

Twilight had set and the skyline looked large, but the same painted colors remained, casting a soft yellow glow on the city. A high stone wall surrounded Amberville, holding all the tightly packed rows of buildings and houses securely inside, and scores of chimneys dotted the rooftops with drifting lines of black smoke.

The pathway to Amberville curved its way down the hillside to the massive gates of the city. It was lined with lanterns suspended on large wooden posts creating a curled line of warm light. To both sides of the road, there were gently rolling hills covered in green grass as plush as carpet. The grass looked almost purple in the low light and it seemed to call the travelers' attention. Hannah was the first to descend the hill and venture into the grass.

"I've missed this place so much. It's beautiful, isn't it?"

Peter stayed on the roadway, still a little unsure. As Hannah moved, fireflies rose up from the floor in swirls like a wake trailing a boat. Peter walked out toward her and his demeanor relaxed when he saw the flickering lights. A tiny firefly fluttered around him and he watched it closely. It dropped onto the top of his hand, flexed its wings, then flickered again.

"My brother and I played here in the evenings. Sitting in the grass. Chasing the lights," Hannah said. She took a deep breath and seemed to inhale the place all at once. Peter smiled. It was an enchanting spot. It felt removed from the darkness of the woods and safe in the shadow of the great walls of Amberville. The air was that perfect temperature, where the skin didn't feel hot or cold and the smell of the short green grass reminded him of another time and place. Another season. Spring. He marveled at his own recollection, surprised that he thought of a different season. It seemed so strange that in this world, where autumn was king, they would find a small spot that appeared out of place, out of order almost.

Mr. Thorne stopped the cart and called after them.

"Hurry! Before they close the gates!"

Hannah sighed. "I hate to leave it. It's been so long since I've felt this way." Peter looked at her and knew by her eyes and her smile that the feeling was happiness. "C'mon," Peter said as he smiled back. They changed course to intersect Mr. Thorne and Master Key on the road just a few yards from the massive gates.

They towed the cart over the threshold just as two strong men closed the big gates behind them. Peter looked down at the cobbled streets then up to the narrow stone buildings that lined the main street. Up above, chimneys puffed smoke back and forth and a trail of dark soot descended and settled onto the street. People were everywhere. An old lady, with a hood concealing her face, brushed by. Peter looked again—the reminder of a witch.

"Well Master Peter, we made it. Welcome to Amberville," said Mr. Thorne as he took in the sights.

"Is this your home?" asked Master Key.

Peter looked long and hard at the rows of houses. He watched the puffing smoke and then pulled his paper from his coat and looked at his old drawing.

"I don't think so," he said.

As the last light faded, the group settled their cart in the Square at the center of the city with the rest of the vendors. Master Key and Peter pitched the tent over the cart and unloaded their goods.

The vendors mixed with a variety of entertainers. There were puppeteers, a group of men clad in metal armor, and lots of musicians. Above the street, Peter could see huge flocks of crows dotting the rooflines and window ledges. Below, he found the cobblestone streets amber under the last streaks of light but Amberville did not glow; it smoked and boiled with a heavy energy that wanted to suffocate.

Hannah was very eager to go to her parents and did all she could to wait until Peter was finished helping set up camp in the Square. She grabbed him by the hand and they ran down a tight alley to another street. They turned and arrived at a tiny house on the corner. There were three pointy cylindrical rooftops that made it look like a miniature castle. Hannah led him down four steps into a doorway that was not much taller than Peter.

Inside, there was a fire in the fireplace with its reaching orange light licking the walls. Peter nibbled on a little piece of peanut brittle, and examined a series of ornamented clocks hanging along one of the walls. He leaned his nose toward a cuckoo clock just as it struck the hour and a small wooden bird jutted out. *Cuckoo!*

Hannah's parents were round, happy people, who were overjoyed to have their child back. They hugged their daughter again and again and Peter was glad to see her reunited with her parents. He could only imagine what they had been through all this time thinking that both of their children were gone. It was obvious that they held their daughter tightly just to make sure she was really there. Peter smiled at the reunion but it felt bittersweet. He could see how happy Hannah was to be home safe and he wished the same for himself. Amberville was like nothing he had ever seen, but it was not home. If anything, he felt like he was further now than he had ever been before.

Hannah sat her parents down at the table in the kitchen. They knew what was coming. She told them the story of the witch and what had happened to her brother. The smiles disappeared and her parents were silent. They cried and tried to comfort one another but strangely, they appeared to accept the fact he was gone. Witches were real and playing in the forest always carried with it the possibility of great danger.

Hannah continued to tell the tale. She described the day Peter came and how he battled the witch and killed her. She told them about Mr. Thorne and Master Key and the weeks they spent at the tree house. Hannah's parents, having listened to the story, turned their attention to Peter.

"Quite a boy," Hannah's father said as he rubbed the top of Peter's head.

"He's a hero!" Hannah's mother exclaimed. "He can stay with us." She pulled Peter close and squeezed him tightly. However, Peter was feeling increasingly uncomfortable with all this attention.

"Yes, yes, he can stay. We have room," her father said.

Hannah looked at Peter and sensed his discomfort. "He is looking for his home." She smiled. "That is, when he's not slaying witches."

"Where do you live?" asked Hannah's father.

"I'm still searching."

Hannah added, "Mr. Thorne said he should descend the hill and go to Port Is-A-Bell."

Hannah's father looked puzzled. "To the faerie islands?"

"He doesn't look like the little people," said Hannah's mother observing the fact that he was quite tall.

Peter didn't believe Port Is-A-Bell was a good idea either. "It was just a thought. Mr. Thorne figured—" Before he could finish, Hannah's mother interjected. "—Well, you'll stay with us."

"Thank you but—"

Hannah's father could tell he was going to object. "—No, no, you must. I insist."

Hannah's mother embraced Peter again. He appeared more uncomfortable watching the reunion shift to him. He found the emotion too much and the pleas for him to stay too demanding. He didn't want to be there. Hannah's parents again begged him to stay, but Peter sensed that they wanted to replace their son and he wanted no part.

"Thank you, but I have to get back to the Square," Peter said firmly. He nodded and walked out the front door before anyone could say anything else. Hannah and her parents were quiet, almost taken aback by Peter's curt farewell.

Outside, Peter took in a deep breath of the night's

cold air and felt relieved. Behind him, Hannah called out.

"Peter? Peter, where are you going?"

Reluctantly, Peter stopped under a street lantern and turned back.

"I'm sorry. I didn't mean to leave like that. It's just that, I can't stay."

Hannah caught up to him. "What's wrong?"

"Look, I'm glad you're home. I'm glad you're safe with your family and I'm very happy for you."

"My mother hugs everyone. A lot. You'll get used to it."

"It's not that…well, maybe a little. It's just…" There was a long pause. Hannah knew what he was going to say before he said it. After her story, she could see what Peter was going through.

"I know. You want to be home."

"And this isn't it," Peter said. "How I can I want what I don't know? I want to be some place I don't remember. Some place I can't even imagine."

Hannah didn't say another word. What could she offer that would make things better? Nothing. Peter turned and walked slowly down the narrow street.

* * *

Another morning. Another day of fall. Peter opened his eyes and studied the direction of the lines in the grain of the wood that made up the bottom of the cart. Everything was quiet in the Square. No voices, just a few light footsteps along the cobblestones. It was peaceful and Peter enjoyed the few moments of calm. It was comforting to simply focus on unimportant details. No responsibilities, no pressures, no chaos, and no threats. But it couldn't last.

Mr. Thorne yelling for Master Key once again broke the silence of morning. Master Key slept down near the wheels of the cart. He woke abruptly and threw his head forward. "Huh? What?"

"Master Key!" yelled Mr. Thorne again.

Master Key blinked his eyes and rose to his feet. Peter looked over and thought that Master Key was probably the only person who could stand upright underneath the cart.

Master Key glanced over and asked "What are you looking at?"

"Nothing," Peter said.

Master Key yawned and slowly stretched acting as though his body hurt.

"Right Mr. Thorne. Work. Work. Work. Always work. You know Master Peter, he could build some better accommodations if he wanted. I miss my little house."

Work started promptly. People shuffled about the Square going from one vendor to the next. Mr. Thorne stood out front and delivered his speech. "Ladies and gentlemen! Fine carpentry here. Fine carpentry found here. Superior workmanship as always." His lines were well rehearsed, but he often got into a rut, and started to repeat himself and used the same tone, which seemed to push customers away rather than attract them. He'd usually drone on for about an hour until no one was remotely near their display.

Mr. Thorne grudgingly came to the conclusion that his stuffy demeanor didn't work well with most of the potential customers, but it didn't stop him from trying. However, he knew it was only a matter of time before he'd turn the show over to Master Key who was quite good at selling. However, Mr. Thorne never let on that this was the case, and often delayed the hand off to Master Key as long as he could. "Slow morning. Master Key, your turn. Give them your best. I am going to take a break." Mr. Thorne wiped his brow with a handkerchief. Master Key crawled up onto a wooden crate set on the platform. This worked much better because the little man was energetic and enthusiastic.

"Come see the finest, the nicest, the very best carpentry Amberville has ever seen! How about you sir? Need a dollhouse for your little girl? She'll love you forever. It has five rooms, each with their own little furniture. Little tiny tables, little tiny chairs! Hours of enjoyment as long as she doesn't try to sit in one."

The Mayor of Amberville, an older man, stuffed into a tight suit, surveyed the vendors. He was red faced with a bushy beard and mustache, and his smile, which he thought was ingratiating, was really more of an off-putting condescending sneer. He strolled along the walk and stopped at Mr. Thorne's display. He listened to Master Key for a moment then fingered and handled the goods set along the front of the cart.

"Excellent work Mr. Thorne, excellent as always," he said in a low muffled voice.

"Thank you Mayor." Mr. Thorne nodded at the approval.

"Come see Mr. Thorne's creations! Splendid creations. Beautifully crafted," Master Key continued. Peter stood near the back of the cart and watched over the inventory. He repositioned a few of the toy soldiers then studied one of the miniature houses, but it was plain to see that his mind was elsewhere. He was thinking about Hannah and her family. He hoped he hadn't offended them too much. They were very kind in their offer but something about it felt all wrong. There was a strange feeling associated with staying there, with staying in Amberville too. It felt like a trap. A prison.

"Mayor, this is Master Peter," Mr. Thorne said.

Peter snapped back from his thoughts just in time to shake the man's hand. The Mayor gave Peter a glance but quickly went back to eyeing the wares on the display table.

Mr. Thorne moved closer to him. "I was wondering if we might have a word with you."

The Mayor turned back with a wooden soldier in his hand, "Go ahead."

"Perhaps at your office?" Mr. Thorne said quietly. The Mayor nodded and continued to the next booth. Peter overheard the request and sensed that he had something to do with it.

Later in the day, Mr. Thorne and Peter left the Square Market and walked through a series of tight alleys. Dusky buildings loomed above with smoke puffing from their chimneys. The dark haze shrouded the orange sky. Soon, they found their way onto a larger street that zigzagged up a small incline toward a stone building at the end.

They ducked under a lamp in the entryway and entered the Mayor's office. It was a huge room with low timber ceilings and a large heavy desk in the middle. The desk was covered with stacks of ledgers, some of which looked dusty and worn, as though they were either archives or long unfinished business. The room was stuffy from the smell of smoke, but it was much warmer than being outside in the Square Market. The Mayor tossed another log into the fireplace and turned his chair back to his desk where he continued to write in a ledger. "So what's this about?" asked the Mayor without looking up.

Mr. Thorne stepped forward. "Master Peter. He's trying to find his way home. Do you know him?"

The Mayor thought about the question and reluctantly took another look at Peter. It took only a few seconds, but the Mayor didn't show any recognition, yet there was a hint of suspicion in his glance. "I'm sorry Thorne, but I can't say that I've ever seen him. I don't think he's one of ours."

Mr. Thorne didn't hesitate to go to his next idea. "Then I was hoping he might gain a place on one of your caravans to Port Is-A-Bell in the morning. I've given him passage for ship travel to the faerie islands."

The Mayor shook his head. "You don't look like little people to me boy."

"So they say," said Peter flatly.

"Then how do you know that's your home?" the Mayor asked Peter in a condescending tone.

"I don't," Peter said.

The Mayor turned his attention back to Mr. Thorne. "Then what do you want to send him for?"

"Well, if he's not from Amberville, where else? He's lost."

The Mayor moved his chair so that his pipe was in reach of his hands. He took a small stick and thrust it into the fireplace then relit his pipe. "What's your town?" he asked Peter.

"I don't know."

"Lost? Lost and stupid. Lost cause Thorne," the Mayor said pulling the pipe from his mouth as though he was tired of talking to them both.

"Even so, can he go with your caravan to Port Is-A-Bell?"

The Mayor smiled at Mr. Thorne's impatience. "Certainly, but there isn't one. Port Is-A-Bell won't let anyone in from this side."

"Why?" Mr. Thorne asked.

The Mayor began to puff on his pipe again.

"You haven't heard? Witches. They've been spotted not far from the city, just yesterday. The whole town is scared. Why do you think business has been a bit slow? Why do you think I was out this morning in the Square Market trying to show people that it was safe?"

"But Amberville's gates are still open."

The Mayor shook his head. "Not for long. We'll close them tonight and keep them closed for a few days. I'm sorry but there's no getting into Port Is-A-Bell."

The Mayor eyed the change in Peter's expression and could see a hint of fear.

Mr. Thorne got up and looked at Peter. "We tried. Maybe in a few days."

As the two stood in the doorway, the Mayor cast another suspicious glance as he thought of something. "What's the boy do?" he asked.

"The boy?"

"Yeah, his trade..."

Mr. Thorne looked to Peter then back to the Mayor. He didn't trust the question, after all, the Mayor didn't seem to care about Peter. Why now?

"He chops wood for me," Mr. Thorne said plainly and then tipped his hat and walked out.

* * *

That evening, as the crowds began to dwindle in the Square, Mr. Thorne went for a walk around the perimeter. There were a few other carpenters who had set up shop and Mr. Thorne wanted to see what inferior craftmanship was nearby competing with his fine works. As he moved by each one, he squinted and frowned and often made low noises of disapproval. He had walked all the way around, back to their own cart, when there was a commotion on the far side of the Square. There were a few gasps and screams and people started moving quickly in different directions. Some people seemed to be retreating deeper into the city while some headed for the walls. Just then a huge swarm of crows flew over the Square. There was a *whoosh* of wind from the thunderous wing clapping and a collective *caw caw* as the birds circled and flew toward the other side of the city.

Peter and Master Key jumped up from behind the

cart and watched the crows disappear from view. Mr. Thorne stood frozen a few feet in front of them.

"What is it?" asked Peter with a ring of alarm in his voice. Mr. Thorne looked again toward the wall, then back to Peter. "I don't know," he said gravely, "but perhaps we should find out. Master Key, stay here with the cart."

"Right Mr. Thorne, I'll stay here, just in case it's something I don't care for much, which something tells me, it is."

Mr. Thorne and Peter made their way across the Square and into a street heading for the wall that already started to loom larger as they got closer. While a few of the townspeople were going the same way, many were heading in the opposite direction, back toward the center of the city.

When Mr. Thorne and Peter reached the end of the street, it split left and right parallel to the wall which was now almost directly above them. Mr. Thorne pointed to a turret a few yards away that rose up alongside the wall. There was a doorway at the bottom of the turret, and inside a circular stone staircase winded its way up thirty feet to the walkway along the parapet. As they climbed the stairs, they could hear voices—a few words here and there from others climbing the stairs above them.

"How could they?" "It's impossible!" "That's what they said!" cried the voices.

Peter wondered about what was said and by who but soon the voices had stopped. A strange hush seemed to emanate from the top. They hit the last few steps and emerged onto the walkway along the parapet. A few clumps of townspeople, along with a few watchmen, stood looking through the notches at the top of wall. They stared transfixed, silent, almost expectant, at something outside of the city.

Mr. Thorne walked down the walkway toward an open notch and looked out over the gently rising grassy landscape, up toward the line of trees that marked the edge of the forest. Peter came alongside and also peered through the notch in the wall. The grassy plain was dark and quiet. Nothing moved, except a few tiny lights from the fireflies that danced over the ground. There was a foreboding silence. No one said anything. They just watched, as though waiting for something they knew would come, something they feared would come. The scene was strangely ominous as there was no apparent danger anywhere, and yet, something wasn't right. Peter glanced to both sides but the plain seemed peaceful as the fireflies flickered and bobbed here and there in the darkness.

And then...all the little lights disappeared. The fireflies went dark and at that same moment, Peter's skin rippled cold with goosebumps. He could feel the hairs on his arms and neck stand straight up. His skin prickled at the sensation and his stomach felt like it dropped into his knees. There was a sound in the forest, at the edge, that almost seemed to correspond with the sensation Peter felt. In his mind, he knew what was about to happen. He could see them in his mind—the witches in the forest. An image growing in his imagination, becoming more defined. The eyes of the witch. The mouth. The teeth. And as her jaw lowered and quivered, a sound…

The cackle of witches reverberated off the hill from the first line of trees. It reached the walls of Amberville like a distorted hungry chant from a pack of predatory animals. The cries were shrill, each slightly different than the next, and they overlapped and created a disturbing call. It was just the sound along the edge of the forest, so clear and loud, but no witch could be seen. The sounds seemed to cut right to the heart of the townspeople along the top of the wall even more. There were the audible inhales but no one spoke. They were frozen with terror. Then there was a new sound, coming up the stairs in the turret. The Mayor stepped onto the walkway, out of breath. He quickly pushed one of the watchmen aside and peered down from the wall and heard the noises.

His eyes grew wide as he said "Witches."

* * *

Later that night, Peter curled up in his corner, under the cart. He wrapped the blankets close and soon the sounds of Amberville diminished and everything went dark. No one was on the streets. They were too afraid. The whole city knew what danger was just outside and their panic was palpable. Peter knew that it only emboldened the witches. He wondered if he would ever escape these creatures. He was tired but his mind didn't want to stop. There was too much to think on. Where would he go now? What would he do? Too many questions. Too few answers. He tried to relax his thoughts and pull the clutching fingers of fear away from his mind. Bend them back and let his thoughts wander to something else.

After a while, his fears subsided and in his mind, he could see a new image. A landscape of trees below him. Then, out of the darkness, the gently curving line of a road. As the landscape got closer, Peter could see leaves flying under his view. Across the road, a house sat in a small clearing. The windows were dark. The tarp on the woodpile whipped in the wind. The shed door was thrown open violently. The bedroom window upstairs was cracked open. There was a bed inside, but it was empty. As the image became clearer, Peter could hear footsteps.

Peter woke to the sound of Mr. Thorne on the other side of the cart talking to someone. He shook as his mind rifled through the fleeting images. Peter rolled over and peered through the tarp.

"Master Peter will not be arrested. He belongs to my party," he could hear Mr. Thorne say. Arrested? Peter's mind whirled. What was going on?

He pulled himself up and crawled to the front of the cart. He could see the legs of men standing next to the wheels. His escape looked clear so he got up and moved to the next cart. Just then two men grabbed him and yanked him back. Peter found himself eye to eye with the Mayor but Mr. Thorne stepped between them.

"Stand back Thorne," the Mayor said in a grim tone. Mr. Thorne looked the Mayor square in the eye but slowly retreated toward the cart. The Mayor, in a long heavy coat, waddled closer to Peter. His cheeks were very red from the night chill. Master Key viewed the scene from under the cart.

"A witch hunter, hmm?" The Mayor eyed the boy carefully but seemed disappointed. "Not very formidable. Not very old. I don't know if you have brought the witches to Amberville or will be the one that saves us all, but you my boy, are coming with me."

"He's not yours to take," Mr. Thorne said. The Mayor stopped then stood toe-to-toe with Mr. Thorne. "Amberville is mine and everything in it. You Mr. Thorne still have some nice valuables here and I'm sure you'd like to sell them."

Mr. Thorne glared at the Mayor but didn't pursue

the issue any further. Master Key emerged from under the cart and rushed after the Mayor but his men pushed him back.

"Peter!" Masker Key yelled and started after them again, but Mr. Thorne stopped him and said, "Wait. Just wait."

CHAPTER TEN

THERE'S NO PLACE LIKE...

It was about midnight and Peter looked up from his jail cell cot. The small room was cold and damp. He closed his eyes, but sleep wouldn't come. He remembered his earlier dream. What was that place? Was that his old house? If it was, why was his bed empty?

"Peter," Hannah whispered. Peter opened his eyes and rolled over. The silhouette of Hannah obscured the moon. She peered down through the barred cell window.

"I'm sorry."

"What are you doing?" he said.

"I didn't know this would happen," she said as she gripped the heavy metal bars. Peter stood on his cot to get closer to Hannah.

"My father was so proud of what you had done, so proud that you saved me." Hannah's eyes welled with tears. "He told everyone about you. How brave you were. I guess the story spread, but I didn't know it would come to this."

"What is it?"

Hannah sighed and looked away. "They think the witches are looking for you. That you're the reason they've come." She glanced down. "It's my fault."

"No, it's not," Peter said with resign. He wanted things to be different. Amberville held so much possibility a few days ago when they arrived, but his path was now clouded from view. There was no journey to Port Is-A-Bell, his pursuers were here, and he was trapped. Somehow, it seemed inevitable.

Hannah pulled herself closer to the bars. "I wish I was in there with you then maybe I would feel safer. I lay awake thinking of witches. When I close my eyes, I see them, and when I open my eyes, they are still there in the dark. If I could sleep, maybe I could escape them."

Peter touched her hand. "What do you dream?" he asked.

"Most of the time, I don't remember but last night, I remember feeling cold. A white dust was falling from the sky and the whole city was covered in it. It was very strange looking."

"Winter," Peter said. "What do you think it meant?"

"I don't know. You know how dreams are. They make sense only when you're in them. When they're gone, they're just pieces of nothing. Remember, lost dreams."

"I remember." Peter smiled to let Hannah know that everything would be fine. She smiled back.

The next morning was unusually cold. A glistening of frost covered the bars on Peter's window. He held himself tightly on the cot and shivered. Not long after, he was taken outside and led to the gates of Amberville. A small gathering of people waited to see Peter's fate. He scanned the crowd but didn't recognize anyone.

The Mayor waited near the gates. He circled the boy and began.

"Whether our city is cursed or blessed matters little. Whether this witch hunter has cursed us by bringing the evil that follows him or whether this witch hunter has blessed us by his services to rid our city of the lurking danger, matters little." No one from the crowd said a word or made a noise. The Mayor turned his attention to Peter and stepped closer. "Master Peter is hereby banished from Amberville for his crime and Master Peter is hereby sent on knight's errand by the people of Amberville to fulfill his task."

Peter stood alone as the crowd watched him silently. Mr. Thorne emerged from the group and went to Peter. "I'm sorry it's come to this." Mr. Thorne appeared uncomfortable, looking as though he might say more but then he stopped himself.

Peter freed him of any guilt when he said, "It's a journey I have to make."

"Go west. You can still make it to Port Is-A-Bell. Maybe find a way in."

"I don't think it's the way home," Peter said.

"Ridiculous, you've been..." Just then, Mr. Thorne stopped and realized that Peter wanted to go in the other direction. "Then go to the tree house. You'll be safe there. Winter's coming."

Mr. Thorne placed a hand on Peter's shoulder and nodded his head. He walked back into the crowd as Master Key approached with a heavy sigh, "This time, I should go with you, even if I don't care for it much."

"It's okay. I'll be alright. You've helped me more than you know," Peter said.

"Here, you'll need this." Master Key handed Peter his hatchet. He gripped it firmly and said, "Thanks Keys."

"Good luck," Master Key said and then returned to the crowd. Hannah was next. She wasted no time. "I want to go with you."

"I'm the one who has been banished. Not you." Peter looked long at her. She touched his cold hand

and said, "Fall has stayed too long. We've forgotten winter." At Amberville's walls, Hannah broke the frost and kissed Peter with a last touch of warmth. She slipped her fingers close and placed a miniature pumpkin in his hand.

"For luck."

"I'll survive."

"How will I know?"

"Your dream of winter will come true." Peter looked long—a promise of the future.

The Mayor stood like a stone as he commanded that the gates be opened. Slowly, the doors *creaked* back and Peter could see the path before him and the forest looming in the distance. As he left the safety of Amberville, the massive gates closed behind him. Everything was still and there was a white layer of frost on the grassy hill leading up to the trees. He looked back once, but then pushed onward.

The forest was dark and the wind blew hard. He could see witch prints on the forest floor from the night before and wondered where the witches were now. Were they waiting just around the next bend? Had they retreated deeper into the woods? He didn't know.

Small branches broke off and fell to the floor. With every step, Peter was haunted by the thought that witches were near. He saw shadows shifting all around, but there were no cackles or calls.

He walked all day and all night with the sensation that hunger was close, but he never wavered, just kept walking. In some places, where the path seemed too quiet, he ran.

The next morning, he passed the cemetery and the pumpkin patch, and knew that he was close to the tree house. After all the cold and darkness, he was falling into despair; the only thought now was getting to the relative safety and familiarity of his former home. He even stopped scanning the woods. Instead, all vision was pointed down the path. Not only was Peter tired from the journey, but he was tired of being afraid. He was nearing a point where, what lay beyond the next tree, was of less concern, or so it seemed.

Behind the next row of trees, Peter heard the sound of twigs breaking.

"Who goes?"

Peter cautiously peered around a trunk and spied a patch of fur.

"I know you," he said.

The squirrel carefully stepped from behind his tree trunk. "I know you," he replied.

"Why are you here?" Peter said. The squirrel shook his fur from head to toe.

"One witch too many. I've seen witches but not a flock, a herd, a pack, a horde of the evil things. No thank you. I'm going this way."

Peter looked over his shoulder, in the direction of

Amberville. "Not much better."

"Can't be any worse. Why are you going that way? Looking for trouble?"

Peter didn't answer. He knew it was not a simple yes or no. It was complicated. The squirrel sensed the trouble and knew that Peter was part of it. He squinted his eyes. "Well, something tells me they're looking for you."

Again, Peter didn't respond. The squirrel moved closer. "You can keep running...or...if you're going that way, you'll find them. So which is it?"

"I'm not looking for witches," Peter said.
The squirrel grinned knowingly. "It doesn't look that way to me, but we each have to face the path that takes us home, and if I remember, you're looking for home."

Peter nodded that this was true.

"Maybe it is that way. Good luck." The squirrel moved along and muttered to himself as he disappeared behind the next line of trees. Again, the forest fell silent and Peter remained in the cold damp woods alone. After a few of hours of walking, at what seemed to be midday, although the diminishing light said otherwise, he could see the beginning of the golden clearing, and a glimpse of the tree house, but something was wrong.

* * *

Mr. Thorne's tree house had been scoured as well as The Great Big Witch could manage. The front door was busted down, windows had been shattered, and furniture had been overturned, at least those pieces that were in reach of the witch's hands.

Peter had little time. Night was coming and he needed to secure the tree house as best he could, for any witch, old or young, big or small. After getting inside the tool shed and finding a few remaining tools, he gathered up stray boards, planks, and anything he could find that might be hammered onto the openings. It took a few hours, but when the sun dipped under the forest's trees and twilight vanished, the task was done.

Inside, Peter found a little food left in the back of the cupboards, mostly dried out bread and corn. He huddled in the darkness, nibbling on little pieces, wondering if he should light a candle. He hoped that no witch had followed and that no one knew he was there, but the condition of the tree house told another story. He made a lot of noise fortifying the tree house and he figured that his racket did not go unnoticed. He could only hope otherwise.

The first few hours were fairly quiet. The only trouble was that if the tree house was always a little drafty and noisy from the wind, it was more so now from all the holes. The boarding up of the door and windows weren't a perfect fit, and the spaces made the inside colder. All Peter could do was keep his clothes and blankets close. One hand was in his jacket pocket holding the small pumpkin Hannah gave him while the other gripped the handle of his hatchet.

After a while, his thoughts moved away from the danger in the woods, and he thought back to the dream he had the night before in Amberville. That other house, the other world. It seemed familiar and yet it also seemed very far away, like a vision or a memory, somewhat real, but everything else saying it was merely a dream. He remembered back to some of his other dreams, but then...

The sound. All night he hoped it wouldn't come. Maybe he was hearing things or maybe what might have been the bone chilling sound of a faint word through a voice box, was something else. He listened, parsing the sound of the wind, trying to filter it out and hear anything behind it. Before, Peter would only think that something was near, but now he knew the sounds they made. He no longer detected "something." He could hear witches.

Wind. Leaves. Trees in the distance. Wind. Nothing else. A moment of relief.

Then, something on the tree, near the door. He listened again, not hearing oil and bile, and no voice yet. It was something rubbing against the wood, something rough...

A lick.

Then Peter saw it from the recesses of the workshop. Movement through the cracks in the boards. A witch, but he was safe. She couldn't get inside he told himself, and she didn't know he was there.

Her bony fingers scratched very gently on the wood. Her nose sniffed the spaces and then it was too late, Peter could see her in his mind. Her terrible form, her writhing body, her protruding face, her straining eyes, her teeth, exposed.

He tried all he could, but it was no use. He was again afraid. How could he control it? Hunger needed to be fed and he was all that stood between a fall of feeding and a winter of death. Peter shuddered in the corner. His skin rippled, and he watched for what might happen next.

To his surprise, the witch was gone. Peter wondered if he was safe. Maybe she thought the tree house was empty. Maybe he had remained hidden, unfound…but that was just wishful thinking.

"Come out Peter…come out," she called in her soothing voice.

Then there were more.

"Peter…"

"I won't hurt you."

There were too many voices to tell how many, four, six, ten? He didn't know but they kept calling him and scratching at the doors, prying at the windows, and licking the spaces. Peter closed his eyes and covered his ears, but it was no use, the sounds just kept coming. They wouldn't relent.

He stayed huddled there, amongst all the cries. He stayed, but nothing happened, no matter how badly he focused on the old dream, this world wouldn't go away.

"It can't be real, it can't be real, it can't be real," he whispered back, but nothing happened.

The witches kept coming. He could hear them pulling boards off and shrieking in delight. They kept coming...were there twenty, fifty? Peter let go and gave into his imagination. There must be a hundred. They all want to eat me, he thought.

Peter looked up and in his mind, he saw the red eyed girl in the cage. She stared long at him. He could see Hannah. He could see her.

Peter sprang to his feet and screamed with his hatchet swinging wildly at the darkness. But just as he swung madly into the kitchen, the witches burst through the tattered boards. The first witch screamed, and it all came back to him—the encounter in the little cottage.

Peter turned and moved back into the hall onto the stairs. He could hear the witches funneling inside, but just as he made it to the second floor, a shadowy shape came across his old room. A huge bony hand swept in front of him, and Peter instinctively dove under it. The Great Big Witch!

Outside, under the moonlight, the hungry witches descended onto the tree house. Little shapes, faster, scampering in through the door and lower windows, and then a large slower shape standing along the tree as though it were a sapling. The Great Big Witch, with her face concealed, searched the rooms, like a hungry mother burrowing her cabinets for traces of food.

Peter escaped the searching hand of The Great Big Witch and sprinted up to Mr. Thorne's room. He slammed the door and locked it. Frantically, he looked around the room and saw the window. The witches brimmed to the top of the stairs and screamed outside the door. *Boom!* The door buckled as they pounded it from the outside. Peter went to the window and kicked it open. Below, more witches. They spotted him and the young ones started to climb the side of the tree. *Boom!* The door fell inward and the attacking hands and fingers swarmed in. Quickly, Peter climbed out the window onto a thick limb. The witches closed from all directions. Peter was trapped.

CHAPTER ELEVEN

SCARDAMALIA

The first witch was just about to grab him when the flying monkeys snatched Peter first and pulled him away from the branches. They flapped their wings and raised Peter high into the sky as the sound of witches faded below.

All was quiet. A thin fog floated over the ground. The trees were dark, gnarled, and bare. Peter huddled near the trunk of a tree. He opened his eyes but felt disoriented. Scardamalia emerged from the shadows draped in her swirling satin blue. Witch-like, she moved toward Peter and her beak-like head craned outward. Noises...*creak, rustle, creak* came from within the hollow witch shell. Some smaller creature was inside. Scardamalia peered out of one of the eye sockets inside the head.

"You're a difficult boy to find. But not so hard now, just follow the witches," she said.

"Yes, you were the one who brought me here," Peter said.

Scardamalia pushed closer but Peter, still very afraid, retreated.

"So it seems. You remember the first night, do you?"

"I know you have been following me. Hunting me," Peter said.

"Searching for you, yes, but not hunting you." Scardamalia continued to encroach until Peter found himself against another tree.

"When are you going to eat me?" Peter asked.

Scardamalia moved down the witch body and peered out another hole in the stomach. "Maybe you don't remember the first night. I'm not a witch." Peter watched the intermittent views of Scardamalia from behind the decayed openings.

"But—"

"—Your imagination runs away with you again," she said. From inside the body, there was a *whirring* and *clicking* of gears and pulleys. Scardamalia's cloak pulled back a few inches to reveal dried flesh and decayed bone—she lived inside the shell.

"See? I'm not very big but this old witch makes a good home. It's much safer for someone like me. I'm not very scary at all. See how you can be your own worst enemy?" Scardamalia opened her arms, letting the cloak swirl around her. "My name is Scardamalia. I want to help you Peter." Scardamalia reached out from a space in the rib cage with a tiny hand. Peter moved closer cautiously and shook it gently. While he couldn't see her completely, she looked much like a small person but her eyes were bigger and her arms and hands seemed longer for someone so small.

"Very good then, we can continue. What has been troubling you Peter?"

"Witches," Peter said.

"Ah yes. Terrible creatures. Like fear itself, they must constantly feed. They scare you?"

"They want to eat me."

Scardamalia pointed instructively. "Don't ponder the thought."

"I try, but I can't help it," Peter said as he checked his arm for goosebumps. Scardamalia saw the gesture and hurried back to him. "What did you do?" Her dried witch face was just inches from Peter.

"Goosebumps."

"How did you know?"

"Hannah."

"The girl. Yes. She too has taught you a few things. Good, good. She's right, don't think about witches. Don't imagine the witches in your mind. They can smell the fear." Scardamalia stared long into the dark misty wood. She spun, whirling the mist with her cloak.

"And what else troubles you Peter?"

"Fall won't end."

Reaching into a pocket, Scardamalia pulled up some dry leaves and let them fall from her tenuous fingers. "Smart boy. Maybe there's still hope. Why should fall end? Witches hunt all year, squirrels get plump and never hibernate. Every day is the same. Today like yesterday. Yesterday like last week. Who's to say, a day, a month, a year, no one remembers. They just keep looking—"

"—for winter," Peter said.

"But it never comes. Where do you live?" Scardamalia asked.

"In the tree house with Mr. Thorne and Master Key."

"Hmm, have you always lived there?"

"I don't think so but I don't—"

"—Where?"

"I'm not sure," Peter said. He looked down as though he was ashamed.

"That night in the forest, what do you remember? Think hard Peter."

Peter looked up at the flying monkeys perched in the branches. "They were chasing me. I could see them fly across the moon."

"That's good, you remember, but before that, what happened?"

"I'm not sure." Peter dropped his shoulders, resigned. Scardamalia turned her back on him while her monkeys took flight from their perch.

"I wish I had found you sooner." Scardamalia dangled her spindly arms up and walked deeper into the woods.

Peter slowly followed her. They walked for nearly an hour until they came upon a swamp. The damp ground slipped under the dark murky water that stretched out in all directions. Clumps of water grasses and cattails poked up from the still pool and the low *croaking* of frogs echoed. Peter noticed that trees grew differently in the swamp. Their roots fingered out over the water creating deep pockets. The flying monkeys circled overhead.

From the water's edge, a narrow raised walkway pushed out across the water toward a small wooden shack that was narrow at the bottom and wider at the top. Up above, it had a small crooked chimney pipe that protruded out of the roof. Peter slowly followed Scardamalia across the rickety walkway that swayed gently from side to side.

Inside the little structure, Scardamalia made a hot bubbling stew in a pot on top of her iron stove in the center of the room. The flying monkeys sat perched in the rafters. A warm firelight glow filled the room. Peter stood in the doorway, tired, but still wary.

"Stew's almost done. Come in Peter, warm yourself by the stove," Scardamalia said.

"I'm comfortable here thank you," he said.

"Mmm. Good stew."

"What's in it?" Peter asked.

"What's it smell like?"

"Pumpkin."

"Yes, yes. Good. Pumpkin stew. You like pumpkin stew don't you?"

Peter didn't reply but his expression said otherwise.

"Who doesn't?" she quipped.

"Witches don't like pumpkin."

"Yes, yes. Come in and have some."

"You have some first."

"Very well." Scardamalia produced a small spoon and dipped it in. She pulled it between two ribs in her witch's body and then she made a long *slurp*. "Ah, delicious."

Peter stepped inside cautiously and sat on a box.

"Eat up," Scardamalia instructed. He took a bowl, filled it, then cooled a spoonful. The first bite tasted good so he kept eating. Scardamalia had another spoonful. "Hot stew. So good when it's so cold out. Cold enough for snow?"

"It never snows," Peter said.

"You could make snow."

"I can't make snow. The weather makes snow."

"Then make the weather make snow."

"I can't do that."

Scardamalia reached out and pinched Peter on his arm. "Ow, what was that for?"

"Either wake up or start dreaming."

"What?"

"I can't tell you. It wouldn't do any good. It will only work if you see it for yourself. See what is happening. When you are awake, your imagination frightens you. When you are asleep, your dreams frighten you." Scardamalia set her spoon down. "Are you safe Peter?"

"No. If this is a dream, then it's a nightmare," Peter said.

"I don't know. Maybe you should go back, hunt your witches, keep your Hannah safe, live in a tree house, and eat lots pumpkin pie. For a boy trying to get home, you have started a whole new life here. Have you forgotten? A whole new life..."

"That's not what I want," Peter said.

"Why not? Isn't this where you belong?"

"No."

"Then where Peter, where do you belong?" she asked.

"Home."

"In the tree house?"

"No."

"Then where?"

"I don't know! I can't remember!" Peter tossed his empty bowl to the floor.

Scardamalia bent down and crept closer. "I should take you up into the sky right now and drop you again but until you see what is happening, you will stay here. I'm only here to help you. Ask the right questions. The answers are yours."

"Are you saying this is my dream?" Peter asked impatiently.

"Are you saying this is a dream?" Scardamalia replied.

"Don't do that."

"Do what?"

"It feels real to me."

"Imagination is a tricky thing when it has power over you."

"Wait, what are you saying?"

"No Peter, what are you saying? Is it possible? Tricked?"

"Tricked. Witches are tricky. They trick to trap."

"Very good. You have made one small step. You see one more piece in the puzzle. Did you always believe in witches?"

"No. I didn't believe in any of this but the days kept passing. I—"

"—Spent some time here, I know. It's hard to

remember after such time."

"Is this why you brought me here?" Peter asked.

Scardamalia sat back down in front of the stew. "Believing in a new world filled with strange creatures, strange people, and strange realities. A place that stays the same only to continue to die the long season of death. Everyone living long lives in a place where the past is just some dark void beyond the woods. We live each day like the last, hoping for a new season that is just around the corner, but it never comes. Yes, our world is in great need. As long as fall remains, the witches continue to feed and grow stronger. But only someone with the power of imagination can change that. Someone not from our world."

Peter stared at her intently.

"You mean...me?"

"Do you remember your own home?"

"Very little."

Peter thought back to the dream he had the night before. The blurred image of his old house. A different world.

"In your world, your powers trap you, but here, they could set you free. They could set us all free."

"What do you mean by worlds?" Peter asked. "Is this a dream or a real place?"

"Now that...is a tricky question," Scardamalia replied. "Dreams are glimpses into other worlds. They are where two worlds momentarily touch...where they echo into one another. Like two leaves falling into water. Their ripples overlapping, reaching each other. It is through your dreams that I was able to find you, in your world, and then bring you here."

"Here? But is this real?"

Scardamalia smiled.

"Do you want it to be?"

"Don't do that. No more double talk. I don't understand."

"It's not double talk. I brought you here because your imagination has power here. You do not come from this place and are not bound by its rules. Unless, you accept this world as your own...then, it will have power over you."

Scardamalia softened her voice.

"It's a lot to take in. I know. But what do you want Peter? To stay in this place?"

Peter thought a moment then shook his head. "I want to go home." He pulled his sketch once more from his pocket and rubbed his thumb over the paper as he remembered. Peter thought about the dream he had the night before. He thought about the image of his house. A different world.

"How? How can you do this?"

"The seasons must change," said Peter.

"Yes, that is why I brought you. You have the potential to gain power through different belief...such as..." Scardamalia paused and leaned in closer,

"...imagination."

Peter thought on this. His mind worked over the words, turning them into images, ideas, then connecting them. He looked back at Scardamalia.

"Fall must end and give way to winter. I will sleep in winter and dream of a different world and will stay there in the world I have been tricked into forgetting."

"How can that happen?" she asked.

"I say it's a dream," Peter said.

"Yes, say it is a dream."

"It is a dream," Peter said in affirmation.

"Then, it is a dream and there is wisdom in how to control it...and escape it. Think hard Peter. Think of that first night. How did you get here? The key is in it."

"But I can't remember."

"You must. Time is running out."

"I can't remember."

"You have to. Our time together has ended. They are coming. Your fears are just outside."

Peter pleaded. "No, you have to help me. You have to—"

"—Remember Peter. Remember. Imagination will help guide you. Control it. Do not let it control you." Scardamalia pulled a lever next to the stove. Gears turned and ropes pulled upward. The roof of the shack opened like a lid. The troop of monkeys flapped their wings and lifted Scardamalia up through the shack.

"Remember, remember..."

"No wait!" Peter yelled after her.

"Come for dinner?" The gnarled grotesque face lunged inward—hands and claws followed. Peter grabbed the pot of boiling stew and threw it onto the witch's face. She screamed and squealed falling inward. Peter ducked her reaching hands and escaped outside. He ran across the raised walkways and could hear more witches beyond the swamp.

When Peter hit dry ground, he stopped and looked around but couldn't determine where he was. Nothing looked familiar to him. He heard witches along the bank and could see moving shapes through the mist so he turned and ran. The woods were dark and damp. He tried to scramble over the slick ground, but he kept falling. Peter picked himself up and stumbled along through the tangled branches. Soon the garbled voices faded behind him and he stopped to catch his breath.

A flash of lightning cut through the fog illuminating something very large in front of him. It was huge and it seemed to tower over all the other trees. Thunder rumbled overhead then another flash of lightning showed that he was in a small clearing.

The first raindrop hit Peter's forehead and he put out his hand to catch another. More lightning and thunder flashed and shook and soon the rain started to come down. As the drops pelted the ground, they pulled the white mist with it. Like a falling curtain, the fog dropped and vanished, revealing an enormous tree. Peter looked up to find three huge trees rising up so high that he couldn't see their tops. Their bark was thick and textured like battle worn armor and their trunks were like hulking pillars that spanned twenty feet across. Peter stared, awe-struck. The three sisters of Three Tree Wood. The very center of the forest.

Another flash of lightning revealed something else—a tall figure, behind the layers of rain. The Great Big Witch. Peter turned and saw moving huddled figures on all sides. Peter ran though muddy puddles while the voices of witches closed in on him.

He was just about to dive between two trees, when right in front of him, a witch screamed. He made a missed swipe at her with his hatchet but another witch, from the side, batted the weapon away. Peter retreated into the small clearing, but he knew that the witches had surrounded him. Old and young, the creatures cooed in their soft voices while others screeched at him animal-like. The Great Big Witch, huge and motionless, watched from the first row of trees.

Rain came in violent sheets and Peter was drenched. He desperately tried to find an escape, but the witches moved closer together. He ran back to one of the large trees and climbed the bottom roots quickly. Soon he was high in the upper branches while the hungry witches circled below. A young witch crawled onto the roots and climbed the trunk of the tree; she would bring him down. Peter saw her and he wriggled out onto a large branch but the young witch continued her pursuit.

Peter closed his eyes. He waited for her to disappear, for him stop believing in the eaters of children. But as soon as he convinced himself that none of this was real, he felt her bony fingers run along his back and her body press closer. He heard the spurious voice she used to soothe him and felt her nose touch his shoulder.

Peter fought the image of what was happening. The image of her. The oil dripping down from her hair and chin. The witch stretching her head to where Peter hid his face. Her mouth opening. The smell of her rank breath. Her teeth dropping down. Her body creeping closer.

Peter shivered. He felt cold. He could feel his skin reacting. Feel the temperature drop. The icy burn. The air was now so frigid and he focused on this. His thoughts stopped racing and soon they converged. A singular focus. A single thought. Cold.

In the garbled voice of witches, she spoke three words...

"Open, your, eyes."

At this, Peter opened his eyes to see her long hand clutching the side of the branch next to him then everything went silent. There was no sound of rain. The drops were gone. Instead, he could see a tiny snowflake gracefully falling to rest on the witch's hand. Another fell and then another, each sticking to the cold skin of the witch.

Crack. The branch broke. Everything slowed. The heavy witch fell first. Peter saw her go under him. He turned over onto his back and could see that the sky above was dark and full of snowflakes. He could feel his stomach sense the drop. The falling.

Then he remembered, this was the way out. The mind fell into the dream and he was trapped, but he was no longer grounded by his fears. The mind no longer accepted the rules of its creation. His will was his own and he wanted to leave unafraid. He remembered the fall on the first night, out of the bag, and onto the forest floor. The way out was the fall...to fall from such a height that the mind couldn't survive.

A swirl of snowflakes moved all around him. The snow...the season was changed. Winter was here. Peter could no longer see the trees. Everything went dark. He knew he was about to hit.

CHAPTER TWELVE

A WINTER'S TALE

Morning came with the sound of a voice. "Peter, it's snowing. Wake up, it's snowing."

Someone was in the room. The air was cold. Peter felt it creeping in over the covers. He reached up and found his ears and head were cold. Lisa pulled his covers back and jumped up and down.

"Look," she cried as she pointed to his window.

Peter squinted and felt disoriented. He put a hand to his head and looked to the window. Lisa grabbed his arm and dragged him toward the view.

"See. First snow," she said excitedly.

Peter looked out. Snow covered the backyard, the

roof of the shed, and the top of the woodpile. "C'mon, get dressed," Lisa said.

"What day is it?" Peter asked, still feeling as though he had slept for days.

"What do you think? It's Saturday!" she yelled as she ran out of the room.

Peter noticed a few leaves clinging to the branch outside his window, then he saw, in his mind, the view from the window of the tree house. He remembered. His mind raced frantically to retrieve the contents of the dream. He sensed its importance and its revelation but the images were fading quickly. They were losing their order. They were becoming random pictures with strange emotions attached. What happened? What was this torn feeling? And like that, the story unraveled.

* * *

That evening, it was time to carve up the pumpkins. Inside the kitchen, Peter's father, Tom, sat at the table with Lisa. Four plump pumpkins were laid out neatly on newspaper. Their father made a triangular shaped cut for an eye in the pumpkin he cradled in his arm. He then turned his attention to the sound coming from the laundry room.

"That you Pete?"

Peter stepped into the kitchen and went straight

to the pumpkins on the table.

"Is this it? Is this mine?" he said. Tom nodded as he glanced down to check whether or not his son removed his shoes. "Your mother is out looking for you."

"I didn't see her," Peter said as he laid his fingers on the surface of the pumpkin inspecting the curve and texture. Tom kept his eyes on his own work.

"It's getting dark earlier so don't stay out so late," he instructed.

"How late?" Peter did not look up. He rolled the big pumpkin on its side and continued to search for the best place to start.

"Definitely before the sun goes down," Tom said.

Peter glanced quickly at his father. "Alright," he said blandly as Lisa peeked over the top of her pumpkin into the opening. She grimaced and turned away. Tom knew what was coming next.

"Dad, I don't want to," she whined.

"You can do it. Just try closing your eyes," her father said.

Lisa wasn't tall enough to sit in a chair and work on her pumpkin. Instead, she switched from kneeling in her chair to outright standing on it since the task required more height. After checking her footing, she took a deep breath, turned her head to the side, and reached down into the pumpkin. A terrible look crossed her face as she pulled her hand out.

"Dad, it feels—" she said as she flicked her fingers wildly to get the sticky sinews off.

"—Look, you carved it, you have to clean it," Tom said.

"But I don't want to," she complained.

"Well, I'm not cleaning all of them."

Peter rolled his pumpkin to a corner of the table where he immediately went to work carving it up. Tom looked over.

"Wait a second, aren't you going to clean him first?"

Peter shook his head to say that he wasn't. His father watched skeptically as Peter made a second incision.

"And shouldn't you use a pen?" Tom asked as he grabbed the first marker his fingers could find. Peter shook his head once more and continued to cut two neatly set eyes. He moved his hand down the side of the face and purposefully carved a mouth complete with jagged turns and notched teeth.

Peter's mother, Susan, came in through the screen door from outside. "Wind's up. And there he is. Peter—"

"—I was just out back. In the woods," he interrupted.

"Well, in before dark," Susan said sternly while she pulled her fingers through her hair to straighten it after the wind had sent it into opposite directions. By her expression, it was obvious she had been looking for Peter for more than a few minutes.

"I know, Dad told me." Peter didn't look at his mother when he assured her that he understood.

Tom leaned back as if he was trying to see out the kitchen window. "Is it going to blow the candles out?"

Susan shook her head, "Where's mine?" Lisa pointed to one of the finished jack-o-lanterns.

"Did you get all the stuff out?" Susan asked.

"The gross stuff," Lisa added.

"Pumpkin guts," Peter said with a smile. He took the last handful of innards from his creation and glopped them into the bowl. Lisa squinted her eyes and stuck her tongue out at her brother. Tom leaned back in his chair and smiled at his son's creation, a neatly cut face with a menacing stare and a large toothy smile.

"Not bad. He's the fastest jack carver I've ever seen."

Susan walked around the table and placed her hand lightly on Peter's shoulder.

"Faster getting in, that's what he should be."

Peter smiled again. He was proud of his creation.

"Seems like you're feeling better," she said to her son as though she was unsure she wanted to bring up the subject. She was happy to see he was more himself again and didn't want it to change.

"I dare you to eat your pumpkin guts," Lisa blurted

from across the table. Peter smiled again, but this time with a sparkle of mischief. Susan got up and went to the sink with a handful of pumpkin soiled newspapers.

"Very funny." She tipped the faucet handle up and rubbed her hands under the water.

Peter continued to stare at Lisa. Abruptly, he looked down and took a fingering of pumpkin mush from the bowl. He lifted it up, pulled his head back, then dropped the orange muck into his mouth.

"Mom!" Lisa screamed.

Susan glanced back. "Peter, spit that out."

"I like pumpkin," he said still trying to chew.

"Well, wait till I make a pie or something," his mother said.

Tom pointed to Peter and appeared little perturbed with the whole scene. "Alright, that's enough. Put a candle in it and take it outside."

Lisa shivered and started to leave the room, but not before singing back, "Peter, Peter, pumpkin eater."

The lanterns were placed on the porch and they flickered in the cold night air. The wind continued to stir and the evening grew late. Leaves danced across the yard and the moon shone high in the sky. Up in Peter's room, footsteps could be heard outside his door. They stopped and his door handle slowly opened. His mother peered in and found...Peter fast asleep.

* * *

However, sleep did not last. Peter awoke later with a sudden and uncomfortable jolt. He opened his eyes and nearly gasped. What was it? His eyes frantically searched the room but nothing seemed out of place. He was alone and everything was quiet. Immediately, his thoughts were about Sarah. If he had been dreaming just moments before, he did not remember.

Peter felt agitated, as though he needed to move. He got out of bed slowly, almost apprehensively. He looked out the window not sure what he was about to find. In his mind, images flashed as he saw the woodshed and the dark trees outside. The image of a red ball appeared in his mind and it made him cold, but he didn't know why he thought of the object.

He went to his window and he inspected it again. It was closed just as it was that morning but now he noticed that it was unlocked. Was it unlocked earlier? He couldn't remember. He looked down and saw something else. There were leaves on the floor. A few tucked into the corner and a few under the bed. Then, his eyes caught something that looked out of place, just under the long drape to the side of his window.

It was a folded piece of paper on the floor tucked neatly under the crease of thick fabric. Probably one of his notes from school he guessed. Something that fell out of his backpack. However, the paper wasn't like the kind he used at school. He reached down and picked it up. It was tattered and rough, almost old looking. His heart pounded. His mind raced. He was about to open it, but something held him back. His mind flashed more images. A tree house. A path. A sky. His hand holding a crude pen. His hand drawing the image of a house. At the same moment, he saw the drawing in his mind, and opened the paper—the same image was on the paper. It was the drawing he made…but it was the drawing he made in a dream.

Peter shook his head. What? No. Now his mind was reeling. He almost felt dizzy and his skin crawled and prickled with goosebumps. It was something he dreamed, but why was this here? Where did this drawing come from? Did he make it in his sleep? He remembered another dream…one where he saw his house from the outside. His window was open and his bed was empty. He was not there. The thought terrified him. Did he dream last night or was he taken? No, it was a dream he kept saying to himself. It had to be. Then, he saw Hannah in his mind clearly. Her eyes, her face, and he immediately thought of Sarah. They were the same.

* * *

Monday. Most of the snow had melted over the weekend but there were still small clumps here and there on the forest floor. The roads were clear and the sun was out; its light cut through the big trees in broad shafts. A school bus slowed and sloshed through the mud and snow on the side of the road. It stopped and Peter stepped off and started his walk home. The bus puffed smoke and then pulled away.

He ventured into the trees and listened. Everything was quiet. He looked around and felt strangely calm, unafraid. He took in a deep breath of cold sharp air and let it out slowly. As he turned, he saw the old abandoned tree house that Sarah had climbed a few days before. He remembered back to their escape into the woods and suddenly he felt a strange feeling come over him. He wanted to see her again and something kept pulling him toward thoughts of her. He wondered why he dreamed of a girl who seemed to be Sarah. He assured himself that that's how dreams were; they were influenced by the things that happened in real life. That's all it was and yet if felt like something more. Much more. He thought back to the dream again and the few images he had from it. A handful of pictures and feelings, but he couldn't make logical sense of any of them. The images were vague, but the feelings were certain.

Peter heard a new sound coming from the other side of the tree house. He followed the sound and peered around the next bend in the path and found Sarah sitting on a stump.

"Are you okay? Are you hurt?" Peter asked.

Sarah turned to see him, her eyes red from crying.

"No," she answered.

"Sad?"

"I came out here to let it all out because I couldn't before. No matter how much I wanted to cry, I couldn't. Until today." Sarah wiped the remaining tears on her jacket sleeve.

Peter stepped closer and placed a hand on her shoulder. She looked at him and smiled then reached over and placed a hand over his.

"I'll be okay," she said.

Sarah got up and took a deep breath, trying to pull herself back together. Again, Peter thought about his dream and held onto the few images he had of the girl who seemed to be Sarah. This moment seemed familiar but he didn't know why.

He wanted to talk to her about his dream, tell her what he remembered, but the desire to do this was quickly crushed by a new fear. What if he told her and she thought he was weird or crazy? The embarrassment would be too much. He had to keep it to himself, he thought.

"You survived," she said.

Peter gave her a puzzled look. He heard her but was still thinking about the embarrassment.

"You made it home on Friday. Nothing got you?"

"Oh, no," Peter said.

"Any nightmares?" she asked.

Peter glanced down and shrugged. This was his chance, he thought. He could share his experience and she might understand.

"Did you use the trick?"

Peter thought for a moment, "The trick?"

"Yes, the one I told you about...to get out? The fall. You'll wake up when you hit the ground." Peter thought again, why did this sound so familiar too? What happened in that dream? How did he get out? Did he fall?

"Maybe. I'm not sure."

Sarah was silent. She looked at Peter and he held her stare. Something touched them both, something connected them. Sarah seemed hesitant but then started.

"I had a strange dream," she revealed. "It was that night. Friday. I only remember pieces. But it was so...real."

A jolt of adrenaline surged through Peter like an electrical charge and it scared him. Was she just saying this to make him feel better about the dreams he had before or had she experienced something similar? How could she? His problem was his own. Why would her dream have anything to do with his? It wouldn't, he told himself.

"You mean vivid?" Peter asked.

"No, I mean real."

Peter swallowed. The words hit him hard. At first, he didn't know what to think or what to say. Sarah took a few steps along the path and glanced back to him.

"Do you want to go for a walk?"

"Sure," Peter mustered.

The cold air cut between them. Winter had staked its claim early but fall was still king. The sun would melt the remaining snow and warm the afternoon hours just enough to push winter back a little longer.

The two seasons had brushed lightly, and the ripples had overlapped. And yet, the two worlds were still close—close enough to echo into one another. A new chorus was about to begin. It was a new song, about to reveal its secrets, its worlds, its stories.

54603851R00112

Made in the USA
Columbia, SC
02 April 2019